A Change of Scenery

By

DEBRA PARMLEY

ISBN -10: 0999252518

ISBN-13: 978-0999252512

Printed in the U.S.A.
First American edition: Belo Dia Publishing August 2017
First short e-book edition: Secret Cravings Publishing 2015
First e-book expanded edition: Belo Dia Publishing July 2017

DEDICATION

To the healers and helpers of this world who are
more about healing their patients than about
corporate profit and who adhere to the first rule of
"do no harm." To the brave men and women who
put their lives on the line to protect our
constitutional rights.

CONTENTS

ACKNOWLEDGMENTS

Thank you to Secret Cravings Publishing for taking a chance on the earliest edition of this story, which was published as a fifty-five-page short. Thank you to everyone who read and reviewed the short story and asked for more – for a longer story, which sparked this trilogy. I'm pleased to be able to do so now through my own boutique press, Belo Dia Publishing.

Thanks to all the editors who have helped with any version of this story and they are: Sarah Biggs, Mikaela Pederson, Heidi Ryan and Tamara Hoffa my first and final editor for this entire trilogy. Tamara took a chance on this story when it was a short and to have her editing the trilogy now feels like the story has come full circle.

Thanks to my beta readers: Charles Welshans and Jocie McKade. Much appreciation to Charles Welshans, my fight scene director and military advisor. All three of the book covers in this trilogy are the work of my talented cover artist, Sheri McGathy. Thank you to Maranda Raven, my PA, who helps me in more ways than I can count. Thanks to my family for their love and support.

To my readers, my fans and reviewers, I appreciate you more than words can convey.

CHAPTER ONE

Atlanta, Georgia, 2015

*A change of scenery—that's what I need. I want nothing
more than to lounge on the beach in the Caribbean and leave the
past behind.*

Clarissa Heat paused in the Atlanta Zuilund Shuttle
Station, dug her ticket out, and took a deep breath. The
place bustled, as if swarmed by an army of ants, each
person clutching a bag while rushing toward their
destination. Something felt off about the terminal today,
but she couldn't put her finger on it. A strange feeling
surrounded her, like everyone knew a secret, except her.
She frowned.

This feeling of being out of the loop—not privy to
the secrets around her—had haunted her since the
divorce.

Joseph C. Heat, the man she now thought of as Joe
Cheat or Cheater Joe, was the cause. Funny how she'd
never put his name together like that in all the time
they'd dated, been engaged, or married. She'd not
known the real Joe until the marriage was almost over.
The ultimate smooth salesman, and for the first two
years she'd known him, he'd been able to talk her into
almost anything.

They'd met after one of her belly dance
performances in Memphis. He'd been charming and
attentive. On the first night he'd issued the smooth line,
"I could lend you my name," with a wink he added,

"Clarissa Heat is the perfect name for a belly dancer." Back then she'd agreed, thinking it way better than Clarissa Small. Now, however, she couldn't wait to change her name to anything but Heat.

Not only had Joe cheated on her, but he'd even slept with the attorney representing her in the divorce. It had nearly knocked her flat. How low would the man sink?

He'd then tried to cheat her out of the home she'd bought with her inheritance and the little bit of money she had left over had gone to her attorney's bills before she fired the bitch for sleeping with and colluding with her husband. It all came rushing back as she stood in the shuttle station, fighting her feelings as people rushed by.

It's no wonder I have trust issues, between my ex and my attorney screwing me over, while screwing each other, but these feelings need to stop. None of these people know me. What kind of secret would they hide? They're just hurrying to catch their flights; they're not keeping secrets. This is ridiculous. Stop it. Remember who you were before you met Joe. Get a grip This is the start of your new life.

She took another deep breath, willed the crazy thoughts and uncomfortable feelings away, and put her mind back on her beach vacation. Hefting her carry-on bag, which jingled from her lucky red and gold coin hip scarf inside, she approached the Zuiland counter and held out her identification card and ticket.

"I was told to check in before our boarding call."

The woman behind the counter took the ticket Clarissa handed her. "Yes, ma'am. We have you on the twelve forty-five flight to Grand Cayman."

"Yes, that's right."

"Good, now if you'll just read this letter," the woman placed a paper on top of the counter, "and then sign here that you've read and understood," she placed a clipboard with paper and pen next to the letter, "then you'll be ready to board. And you'll go through the line to your far right."

Clarissa looked over to where the woman pointed. A long line of passengers, many of them reading books or magazines on those floating red hoover movers which floated in the air in front of their faces, had lined up to wait behind a short partition, while three nurses were busy giving shots. She frowned at the thought of shots and looked down at the letter.

Zuilund Shuttle Line

HEALTH NOTICE

In the past few weeks, we have seen new reports of gastrointestinal illness on some shuttles and on land. Concerns that a new X5W3 strain may spread rapidly have caused us to take new precautions. X5W3 is highly contagious and can be serious for some people.

The gastrointestinal illness symptoms include vomiting, diarrhea, severe dehydration, and can result in death. If you begin to experience symptoms consistent with gastrointestinal illness, we ask that you notify one of our staff immediately. A member of our medical staff will examine you and provide treatment.

As a precautionary measure, to protect our passengers and crew, we now require everyone boarding our international shuttles to take a Sendot immunization, which protects you from contracting X5W3. This is for your own safety. This will have no impact on the quality of your flight, the injection will take less than one minute and carries no side effects.

*Upon receiving Sendot, normal boarding procedures
will follow. If you have any questions or concerns,
please contact a staff member. A nurse from our
medical department is available to answer any medical
questions you may have. Thank you in advance for
your cooperation and understanding.*

Clarissa frowned and tapped her newly manicured
red nails on the counter as she thought.

There always seemed to be some new health
directive issued by the CDC. TV commercials were full
of warnings about taking any over-the-counter
medicines or any drug without the new orange and black
FDA rating symbol, which reminded her of a pumpkin
with two stripes down the middle. Fewer over-the-
counter medicines were being sold and new prescription
drugs were touted as being better than anything non-
prescription.

At twenty-nine, Clarissa was old enough to
remember a time when people took whatever they
wanted, and prescription drugs were the only thing
under any sort of control. Now things had changed, but
some people still grew medicinal herbs in their
basements, where they could remain undetected,
including Clarissa. She knew a lot more about herbs
than pharmaceuticals. Briefly she thought about the
herbs growing in her spare bedroom and then pushed
that thought away and pondered what to do now. She
couldn't chance taking some new drug she'd never taken
before and then boarding the shuttle. Not with her
history of drug allergies.

The woman at the counter gave her an impatient
look. Clarissa gave her a smile but kept her thoughts to
herself.

Best to simply sign the form and be done with it. Don't say a word, and don't draw attention to myself.

Still, she couldn't help but feel nervous as she signed the form, but then she pushed her feelings aside, gathered her bag and headed for her gate.

Passengers who'd passed the checkpoints moved along paying no attention to each other as their red Hoover Movers floated in front of their faces. She'd never seen so many of the bobbing red things in one place before. They seemed to be everywhere. Like the red apples bobbing in a game barrel at a Halloween party she'd attended as a child, these red notebooks bobbed around in the air.

Clarissa missed real books you could hold in your hand and turn a page and she missed real movie theatres, with their smell of popcorn and crowds of people laughing together. She'd resisted buying a Hoover Mover.

The Hoover Company had come a long way from the days of her aunt's vacuum cleaner, which hoovered across the floor picking up anything in its path. Clarissa still read books she could hold in her hand and turn the pages and she went to antique book stores to buy them. So many of the bobbing devices moving about the shuttle station gave Clarissa pause. She just couldn't get used to so many of them floating through the air. At least they weren't all playing music or movie sounds to compete with the shuttle station announcements. It was noisy enough in here.

She paused to read her ticket for the gate letter and number when a large woman pushed Clarissa into a trashcan. She looked up in surprise at the flamboyant woman, decked out in a black dress with a purple turban on her head, before landing flat on her ass, the coin belt in her carry on jingling. Not seeming to care or notice what she'd just done, the woman ignored Clarissa. The woman reeked of garlic and onions. Rude and smelly. Never looking back, the woman continued pushing her way through the crowd. The strange feeling that something odd was going on returned.

What is with all these people? They're full of anxiety. This was a big shuttle station, though, and maybe that's all this was, everyone full of anxiety. *Maybe it's just me, and I'm off.* Still, as she reasoned, the feeling persisted. A man in orange tennis shoes walked passed and she drew her feet back so he wouldn't step on her toes. Little black sandals had perhaps not been the best choice to wear to the shuttle station if people weren't going to watch where they were going. She looked down at her red manicured toenails and wished she'd worn other shoes.

The loudspeaker crackled. "Attention, all passengers, check in at your gate immediately upon arrival. All passengers must sign the release form and receive Sendot before boarding."

She had to be careful when taking any new drug, because she'd had horrible reactions to several of them before. She glanced at her medic alert bracelet, which contained the list of things she couldn't take.

"Passengers without Sendot will not…" A flashing cart driving down the middle of the terminal drowned out the rest of the announcement. Clarissa stood, dusted herself off and shook her head as she looked after it. The man in the orange shoes was across from her on the other side of the walkway, looking at her and then he looked at the cart too. The cart had a yellow sign on the back, which read "Sendot" in red letters.

She didn't feel right about the mysterious drug, and she didn't like that she hadn't been told about it earlier.

These changes were making her nervous. She could've sworn she saw large guns in the cart with the two men wearing helmets. No, I must be seeing things.

Yesterday at the eye doctor, they'd put drops in her eyes to dilate her pupils, because their computer eye scanner system was out, so they had to resort to the old ways, using drops from a dusty bottle stored in an antique cabinet that was mostly in the office for show. The elderly receptionist had reminded the doctor that he still had his father's things in that cabinet. Most of the doctors in practice today came from a family of doctors as those professions had become entirely a who you know kind of thing. So the old doctors meds were still in that cabinet and something was off with that solution. It was so old. Maybe they shouldn't have used that on her eyes. She'd had to wear sunglasses until the meds wore off. Maybe they hadn't completely worn off and were still in her system, doing God only knew what. She could be having some kind of delayed reaction, making her see things, who knew, with the way her body sometimes reacted to drugs.

Men don't ride through shuttle stations holding automatic weapons, at least, not here in the U.S. Only military police were authorized to carry big, automatic weapons. Was airport security now part of the military police?

That wouldn't be much of a surprise, as the mergers had begun a few years ago when riots had broken out in fifteen cities. With local police forces strained beyond their capacity, most citizens were relieved when National Guard troops were sent in. Clarissa had been very uncomfortable, however, when those troops not only arrived, but also stayed. She'd had a strong feeling they'd never leave. Her intuition proved true when National Guard troops from each state later merged permanently with the local police departments. Now there was only the military police. No city police or local sheriff positions existed any more. She supposed they'd now taken over airport security too, and she tried to remind herself they were supposed to be the good guys.

Oh, who was she kidding? This was martial law, however you wanted to look at it, that one fact did not change, and it did not sit well with her.

"Attention, all passengers, check in at your gate immediately upon arrival. All passengers must sign the release…" The repeating message had an obnoxious quality. Was it going to repeat every few minutes?

She tuned the loudspeaker voice out as best she could and turned her thoughts back to Sendot. Unlike most people, she didn't take medicines blindly. Clarissa decided to find out more about the vaccination and explain her medical history.

Clarissa hefted her shoulder bag and collected her carry-on. Her mouth was dry, probably from nerves, and she headed to get something to quench her thirst before talking to the nurses. The man in the orange shoes turned the other direction and walked away from her when she looked directly at him.

When she entered a room labeled "Lounge," the heavy door slammed behind her. Darkness enfolded her and sudden panic rose in her throat. She spun and grasped the door handle, tugging hard, but it didn't budge. She was locked inside the dark, empty lounge and her thoughts raced.

Oh no! Where is everyone?

With her balled fist, she pounded on the door. "Help! Let me out!"

After several minutes of pounding and yelling,

however, it was clear no one would help her. She heard only silence. No annoying loudspeaker, beeping cart, hurrying people, no floating red hoover movers with people blindly following them and no chattering voices—nothing but dead silence. If she couldn't hear anyone, there was no way they could hear her.

As Clarissa's eyes adjusted to the dark, she took in the room. The upholstered seats of the club chairs were shredded, and foam stuffing, overturned tables, and broken glass covered the floor, along with empty bottles of Sluthe, that energy drink so many people liked.

Clarissa couldn't stand it. That stuff would hop you up like speed so you wouldn't be able to sleep for two days. Sure, you could get a lot more done because you could stay up for sixty-eight hours, but then you'd eventually crash unless you drank more of it. Too many people were now addicted to the stuff since it came out two years ago. A city full of Sluthe drinkers had changed everything. Everyone was in more of a hurry, and people expected things done faster. The worst thing was the crime rate had risen and never come back down. Still, the stuff was legal and sold in most stores. Crazy.

She reached a finger out to touch one of the torn chairs. A dry white substance coated many of the surfaces, and an odor she couldn't place assaulted her nose, which stopped her from actually touching the chair seconds before her fingertip made contact.

Oh wait. What the hell is this stuff? Did they spray something? Maybe that's the smell. No wonder they kept the door locked, something odd must have happened here.

She backed away from the chair. They'd closed this lounge to repair it, but now that she thought about it, the door hadn't been locked, or she couldn't have gotten in. Had someone locked the door behind her, or had the door been set to lock itself? Her thoughts tried to rise to a panic again.

Who will know I'm locked in here? I'll miss my flight.

She forced her mind to stop racing, but was then filled with aggravation.

So much for my restful getaway in the Caribbean, lounging on the beach. This isn't the change of scenery I was looking for.

She pulled out her cell phone to call the Atlanta shuttle station. Surely they'd send an employee to get her out.

No service.

Clarissa stared at the only light in the room, where her screen showed no bars, and wanted to scream.

After plunking down on the floor where there wasn't any white powdery foam covering the surface, she leaned back and closed her eyes.

Can it get any worse? No, don't even go there. She knew it could always get worse, she'd learned that from Cheater Joe. *Never think 'can it get any worse.' Never ever think that because that is exactly when it does.*

A tear ran down her cheek, but she was too tired to wipe it away. Damn it, she needed this vacation. She wanted to be relaxing on the beach, not stuck between home and her destination, locked in a room, with no one knowing she was missing.

****

Warren West cracked open the door, eyes scanning the supposedly deserted lounge before slipping inside. As a Navy SEAL his training made him aware of his surroundings and kept him always vigilant.

A woman was sitting on the floor of the destroyed lounge against the wall where it didn't appear the Rida foam had been sprayed. No traces of the white powder were near her or on her. Good thing, too, as even the remnants could cause a chemical burn.

He watched the alluring curves of her chest rise and fall.

Alive and breathing. Good. Now why is she sleeping here? Or is she unconscious?

He clicked his flashlight to a lower lumens setting and pointed the light close enough to see her and assess if she was wounded without waking her.

Her head leaned to one side, and soft waves of blonde hair covered her face, curves like those of the nineteen-fifties film stars. She wore a white blouse with red polka dots, red polished toenails, thin black sandals, and red lipstick upon full lips. Her poster—the antique kind his grandfather had on the wall in the garage—could have read "Sleeping Pin-Up Girl."

Why is she in here? Did she slip inside to sleep or to hide from someone? He wondered if she'd tried to avoid taking Sendot, and if so, how aggressive the airport security would have been with her.

He stepped closer and knelt to examine her. Her breath came slow and even through soft, full lips. Lips that tempted him to kiss her. His gaze lingered on her lips and he thought of kissing her, how that might feel and how she might taste. Everything about her appeared soft and touchable, yet untouched. There were no signs of bruising or ill treatment that he could see.

Warren breathed in her enticing scent, an exotic perfume, perhaps. Finding her here was like coming upon a flower in the midst of war-torn rubble, a reminder of what was beautiful and good in the world. This was one reason he'd fought, to protect all that was good in the U.S.A.

Her lashes fluttered and her chest rose on a sigh. Tear tracks streaked down one side of her face. *What had she been crying about?* He wanted to touch her and wake her to ask if she was okay. He wanted to wipe away those tears and kiss her until she forgot them. Warren sat back on his heels.

No. This isn't the time or the place for making love to pretty girls. Even pretty girls with kissable lips. And tempting as it is, you couldn't go kissing a girl unless you knew she wanted to be kissed. Few women welcomed a kiss from a complete stranger when they're sleeping. This isn't sleeping beauty. Though she is beautiful.

She turned her head away and moaned, then repeated the motion and sound.

She's having a bad dream. Should I wake her?

He wanted to comfort her, but he didn't make a move. Some women weren't as innocent as they appeared, and he didn't know her. There it was again, though, tugging at him, that hero to the rescue habit he'd sworn off. The last time he'd saved a woman, she'd turned around and shot him. The wound had healed, but it had left a scar and a well-learned lesson.

She awoke, startled, and opened her mouth to scream.

His hand closed over her mouth before she could make a sound. "Hush. You're safe. I'm not going to hurt you." He gazed into her eyes, reading her panic. "No screaming." She looked back at him through wide, fearful, green eyes. They both paused, watching each other, cautiously. Something shifted between them though, and it told him she wouldn't scream. "I'll move my hand now. Be calm."

She gave a slight nod, and he removed his hand and waited for her to speak.

"How did you get in here?" she whispered, her voice soft and low.

"I opened the door." He smiled, hoping it would reassure her.

"Smart aleck." Still serious, she frowned slightly.

He couldn't resist teasing her, and his smile deepened. "Isn't that how you got in?"

"Yes," she answered slowly, as if he'd dragged the word out of her, and frowned deeper.

So, this is the way it's going to be. Her eyes held mistrust. Teasing wasn't going to make her relax. "Why are you in here sleeping?"

She gave a great sigh and spoke, "I saw the lounge sign and came in for a quick drink before checking in at my connecting gate." She glanced around, as if looking for something. "What time is it?"

"Six PM."

"Oh no! I really have missed my flight. I can't believe this." Her shoulders slumped. "The door locked behind me and I couldn't get out. I yelled, but no one heard me. My phone has no service here, so I was stuck. Damn it, I don't think my ticket is refundable. I should be in the Caribbean already. I had a twelve forty-five flight."

"Missing your flight today was a good thing. I'm glad I found you in here before they found you."

Clarissa frowned. *This did not sound good. Who is he talking about? What does he mean missing my flight is a good thing?*

CHAPTER TWO

A good thing? Clarissa couldn't help but frown again. *How can he say that? Is he flirting with me?* She wasn't in the mood to be picked up by some stranger in the airport, even if he was tall, dark, handsome, and well built.

"This is a good thing, believe me," he repeated, "be glad you aren't on any flights out of the U.S. today. You don't want to take the Sendot immunization they're giving—it isn't what they're claiming it is."

"What in the world are you talking about? And, for that matter, who are you?"

Yes, who are you, Mr. intriguing, handsome, conspiracy man? Drawn to him despite the circumstances, she couldn't help but wonder just exactly who he was.

"Warren West and I know quite a bit about those injections."

"I'm Clarissa Heat."

"Clarissa," he smiled back, his deep brown eyes searching hers, drawing her in. He reached out his hand to pull her up.

She grasped his hand feeling its strength and warmth as he pulled her up, as she stood. Standing beside him, she realized how much taller he was; at least six-feet tall to her five-foot-five. A deep longing from her belly all the way down to her toes rose at the thought of his warm hands touching her body. His voice saying her name still resonated deep inside of her.

Lost in his eyes momentarily, she forgot to ask the question that had risen in her mind. "What do you know about those injections?"

"Sendot, the so-called vaccine the company is forcing all passengers to take before boarding any of their shuttles leaving the country, is not a good thing."

"What do you mean?"

"They're saying it's a preventative injection for a new gastrointestinal illness."

"I hadn't even heard of it until today."

"Don't you watch the news?"

"Not anymore. I have enough going on in my life without hearing more bad news. I don't follow the news much."

"It's mostly lies and half-truths, anyway, you aren't missing real news. You must not get out much. What do you do for a living, Clarissa?"

"Well, I'm...um," she hesitated, knowing how men changed their attitudes toward her once they knew of her job. "I'm a belly dancer with the Blue Nile Troupe. We dance at the Harem Lounge in Memphis, Tennessee."

"Interesting. Clarissa Heat, the belly dancer. Is that your real name?"

"Unfortunately, yes, until I get it changed."

He didn't seem to react after hearing about her job. There was no change in his eyes. She watched him as her thoughts processed this realization. *I guess he's not impressed. Well, at least he's not leering, coming onto me, or telling me he wants to marry me. That should've been a red flag with Joe.*

Warren's lack of reaction was a first, and she didn't know what to make of it.

"I'd have placed you as more of a pin-up girl or a model.

"My grandmother was a pin-up girl a long time ago. I like retro things and history."

"I enjoy history as well if the books are prior to twenty thirty when they started taking the truths out and rewriting everything."

"I do too. I like old books, the kind with pages."

"Expensive to get, but worth the expense."

"I agree. I don't like the way the electronic books can be totally changed from one day to another the moment the government says switch them."

"That's too much control, I agree. Speaking of control, did you sign the letter they gave you saying you would take the injection?"

"Yes, I signed it. But then I came in here and got locked in and missed the injection, and my flight and you know the rest from when you came in and woke me."

He stood and reached for her hand. "Come on, I have to get you out of here, now."

"Why, what is so urgent? I've already missed my shuttle."

"Missing your shuttle they won't care about, but

you didn't take the Sendot injection after signing the form, and that they will care about. They're likely looking for you now, because they'll want to know why you didn't take the injection and why you disappeared."

"Well, I can't take it." She held up her wrist with her medic alert bracelet. "I've had very bad reactions to several drugs, so I'm not blindly taking anything."

"Good. What are you allergic to?"

"Too many drugs to mention. I don't take anything, except Penicillin, if I have to. When they prescribe stuff, I just throw the paper away."

He frowned deeper this time. "Then you'll already be on their list as a possible rebel and terrorist. They track that kind of behavior." His eyes narrowed as he thought. "They may have been watching you when you entered the shuttle station. Now you'll also be on the newest CDC list—and you don't want to be on that list."

Alarm filled her. The CDC had an enforcement division and would swoop into a town if they thought a new disease was spreading. The image of their grey uniforms with red crosses and the large black guns they carried made her shiver and her thoughts returned again to the herbs she had stored at home.

What if they go into my house and find my bedroom with all of my herbs and seeds? They'll arrest me on the spot.

Her eyes widened and she shouted. "I'm no terrorist!"

"Do you grow herbs? In your basement?"

She hesitated. "I don't have a basement."

"You didn't answer my question."

Oh, God. She eyed him in silence, weighing whether to tell him. She certainly did not have herbs in her basement. He hadn't said bedroom, where she did have them, so she said, "No."

"You're a terrible liar."

She sighed. "I know."

"You also have the look of perfect health, most growers do. Your rosy cheeks are a dead giveaway. Does anyone else know? Are you connected with any other growers?"

His gaze made her feel as if he could read her inside and out. She hadn't known there were other growers or that they were even called growers. "No." She shook her head, breaking the intensity she was feeling. "It's just me. I keep to myself."

"You're sure?"

Exasperated, she answered quickly. "Yes, I'm sure. I didn't know there were others like me. My aunt passed her seedlings on to me before she died and she left strict instructions to keep the knowledge in the family."

"Good. Okay, we have to move. You've been in this room too long already. That super shuttle only takes fifty minutes to get to the Caribbean from Atlanta; they'd have started looking for you once your flight took off without you. If they catch you here, they'll detain and question you, and we don't want that."

"Who? The CDC?"

"No, the DPIV."

She gave him a questioning look. "The what? I hate
19

all these acronyms."

"Deputies of Public Immunization Verification. It's new."

"Wow, that's a mouthful. I've never heard of them."

"As I said, it's new. They have broad-ranging powers, and they've made it so no one can fly out of the States without receiving Sendot. They have the right to detain you if you don't. They're not letting anyone out without it and they'll be tracing you."

"I don't like the sound of that."

"Neither do I. It's just the start of a plan to inject every American with Sendot whether they like it or not, and that goes against your rights as a free American. You're still free, no matter what anyone tells you. Did anyone touch you, handle your carry-on, or bump into you after you entered this shuttle station or Memphis station?"

"Well, there was a lady who knocked me into a trashcan, as if she hadn't seen me. She didn't even apologize. Some people are so rude."

"I'm going to have to search you and your carry-on for bugs."

"Really? You've got to be kidding."

His stance and look told her he was far from kidding.

"I'm not taking my clothes off for you."

She wasn't going to strip down in front of a man she'd just met and knew nothing about. Stripping was what her mother had done before she'd been shot at the

Pussycat Club in Memphis when Clarissa was ten. Raised by her more modest and extremely religious aunt Lyndsay, Clarissa had vowed to never be a stripper, even though she loved to dance. The men her mother brought home from the strip club hadn't been good men. Clarissa was never going to be like her mother.

"Do you have any other clothes in that carry-on?"

"Yes, of course. A sundress and my swimsuit for the beach."

"Good. Change into that dress."

"I told you, I'm not taking my clothes off. I'm a belly dancer, not a stripper."

Dance was freedom. So, although her aunt had forbidden it, Clarissa would sneak dancing when Aunt Lindsay couldn't see her. After much practice, she'd become a professional belly dancer. She wasn't about to start stripping, now. Bad things had happened to every stripper she knew. But with belly dance you never had to take off your clothes and you could keep your distance from the men. Stay up on the stage and the bouncers made sure none of the men touched you.

Warren turned his back to her without responding and moved toward the door before he spoke. "Hurry up. I won't look. The sooner you change, the sooner we get out of this room." He reached into his backpack and pulled out a black tool, which he unfolded before applying to the door lock.

She was taken aback by the fact that he seemed to show no interest in seeing her naked. Most men, upon hearing she was a belly dancer, were all about getting her into bed. Warren wasn't treating her any differently than he had before she'd told him she was a dancer.

While his back was to her, she changed into the yellow sundress. "If everyone has to take this Sendot before they fly, why didn't they make me take it in Memphis on the first shuttle?"

He spoke over his shoulder, "The only people who have to take the injection right now are those leaving the country. They claim it's an international issue and keeping the illness inside our borders is their first goal. But we know the CDC lies." He continued watching through the cracked door. "Ready?"

"Yes, I'm dressed."

He turned and gave her a head to toe glance before smiling. "Good."

Self-consciously, she ran her hand across her hair and wondered what to do now. Too shy to speak, as he watched her, and not knowing what he was thinking, she swallowed and then gave him a small smile in return.

"I still need to search your carry-on, and you, but it will be easier with that dress on."

If he needs to search my clothing for a bug, why did I need to change clothes?

"I wasn't wearing this when she bumped into me." Her eyes narrowed. "Why can't you just check the clothes I took off?"

He shook his head. "The new bugs adhere to your skin. You'd never notice them."

Skeptically, she raised one eyebrow. That didn't seem plausible. "Really? You have no idea how sensitive my skin is."

"Just like you wouldn't feel a tic, you wouldn't feel

this."

She still remained hesitant.

"These work like a bug, except that they're light, transparent, and sticky. If you even felt it, you'd just think you brushed up against something sticky. A chemical in it mixes with your body heat to show up on their scanners so they can track you."

"That's crazy."

"That's the new technology. You'd be surprised at the lab projects they have in the works."

"Okay." She let her tension go with a sigh. "Check whatever you need to check."

He walked over to her carry-on and had her open it. Inside was her beachwear, a pair of jeans, tennis shoes and socks, her lucky red and gold hip scarf, and a silk veil in red and gold swirls. Makeup, gold bangle bracelets, and hoop earrings were jumbled together with her things, as if it had all been tossed in at the last minute.

Looking at the colorful mess and the pink panties that had now tumbled to the floor, she blushed and cleared her throat. "Well, there it all is."

A jumbled mess…like my life.

He rummaged through, looking at one thing and then another, examining everything thoroughly. When he jingled the coins of her scarf, she explained, "That's my lucky hip scarf."

"Interesting." After he placed everything back inside and flipped the flap closed again, he said, "Nothing here." He then stood, looked at her with those deep brown eyes, and with a calm and commanding voice, he said, "Come here."

Damned if she didn't want to do just what he said. There was something about his voice that reached deep inside her. She stepped closer as his steady gaze stayed upon her. She barely knew him, yet he drew her like the tractor beam from an old movie she'd seen.

The moment she stopped in front of him, he said, "Hold your arms out."

She complied, tempted to say, "Yes, Sir." His voice of command was just that compelling. Yet she resisted saying it and only thought it. He turned his gaze and hands to searching her. Her pulse increased and her breath changed as, inch-by-inch, his fingers moved over her skin and her body longed for more of his touch.

Warren exercised the utmost care in touching her skin in his slow search for a bug. His warm fingertips were gentle across her skin, which was brought alive with the sensations. He stopped, as if he knew she was aroused. He closed his eyes, took a deep breath, opened them, and stood.

She caught her breath. He was done, so she needed to be, too. *This is crazy. No men, just sand and beach*, she reminded herself.

His gaze was intent upon her when he spoke. "No bugs."

"Oh, good." Her voice came out breathy and she blushed, looking away from him to break the building tension. "The woman who bumped into me was probably just some foreigner who didn't know what she was doing."

"Maybe, but I had to be sure."

She nodded, but had trouble looking back at him. Her skin was alive with sensations brought to life by the touch of his fingers. He was so close and so male and his eyes seemed to see inside her. Yet she didn't know him. This kind of intensity could be dangerous with a man you didn't really know.

He spoke, breaking the awkward silence. "Do you have a boyfriend? Been dating anyone?"

"No, I'm divorced. I haven't met anyone I wanted to date since..." Watching him her first thought was, Until now.

Warren watched her, taking her in, and nodded as if he'd decided something. Instead of asking her to complete her sentence he said, "When we go out there, we're going to pretend to be a couple."

"What?" His words threw a dash of cold reality at her.

"They believe you're travelling alone, so they won't be looking for a couple."

She frowned. "How would they know I'm travelling alone?"

"They run background checks once you buy a ticket, and they pay attention if anyone is travelling with you."

"That gives me the creeps."

"It's the information age, sweetheart, and information is power."

"I still don't like it."

"Being informed is better than not. It's safer for you."

"How do you know all of this? Who are you, Warren West?"

He turned and looked at her with intensity as his eyes searched hers, as if deciding whether or not to tell her. Then seeming to reach a decision, he spoke, "I'm a member of Deep Nest."

"Never heard of it."

"You wouldn't have, and you aren't hearing this now. I need you to trust me right now. Will you trust me?"

They watched each other for long minutes as she mentally debated before she finally nodded.

"Don't make me regret this," she warned.

"You won't. Deep Nest is an underground group of former and current Special Forces."

"Are you wanted?" She gasped and put her hand to her chest. "Are you a spy or a mercenary?"

"No, and no. Just a Navy SEAL who swore to defend the Constitution against all enemies, and who will defend you."

A Navy SEAL, he's one of the good guys. She exhaled a breath she didn't know she'd been holding and let her hand drop. "I'm glad."

"You'll be safe with me. Now, trust me to get you out of this shuttle terminal." She nodded. "I need you to follow my directions exactly, and without question. Can you do that and also appear calm?"

"Yes, I think so."

"If anything happens and we're separated, keep

going. Get out of this shuttle terminal. If they take you, don't accept the Sendot injection. Tell them you're phobic, scared of needles because of your drug allergies. Have a screaming fit on the floor when you see the needle or whatever you have to do, but don't give in quietly."

"Okay." She blew out a breath. *That will be easy.* "I was already planning to refuse. One reaction I had to a drug nearly killed me. What exactly does Sendot do? What's in it?"

"There's not enough time to go into everything, I'll tell you later. Right now, I want you to pretend we're in love and can't keep our hands off each other."

She raised an eyebrow and watched him. *Does he think that line will get me into bed?*

"We'll blend in with the crowd easier that way. If I need to hide you, I may kiss you fast. I need you to be okay with that. More than okay, I need you to make it believable."

"Okay…" She was reluctant, but at the same time, her heart thudded. Her gaze settled on his lips as she thought about him kissing her. The thought of him not being able to keep his hands off of her, the thought of his kiss, made her all warm and tingly. But they didn't even know each other. Not really. So, she had to stop that line of thinking right now, before she got into trouble.

"Wait," she placed her hand on his hard bicep and he glanced down at her, "I'm not sure I can pretend to be in love. We just met a few minutes ago. You're a complete stranger."

"You're a belly dancer." He smiled. "You should know how to pretend, to create an image. You can pretend if it means you'll be safe."

She nodded. Cheater Joe had taught her not to trust men. So, although her body reached for the handsome SEAL, neither her head nor her heart were fully on board, yet.

This is only desire, strong, magnetizing desire. I can pretend. I can do anything to be safe. She had to remember that pretending was all this would be though. None of this was real. They would just be pretending.

"Besides," He smiled deeper this time. "Don't you believe in love at first sight?"

Her heart wanted to. She very much wanted to believe. But she didn't answer him. To tell him the truth would let him see into her heart. Where she very much longed for love at first sight and a happy ever after.

His hand reached for hers, and his fingers threaded through, strong and warm, sending tingles up her hand and arm. He winked.

She couldn't help but respond with a smile.

"Come on, then," he said. "Let's go."

They exited the room and closed the door behind them. Just then, she heard her name and jumped. "Passenger Clarissa Heat, report to the shuttle security office. We have your updated ticket." Panic filled her. *Oh my God, they really are searching for me. Updated ticket my ass, it's a trap.*

What if someone recognizes me before Warren gets me out of the shuttle station?

CHAPTER THREE

Dread filled her, eyes wide, chest tightening.

"Calm down and breathe." His voice helped her to calm her racing heart. "Start walking." Warren slid his arm around her waist, his hand warm against her side. His strength was comforting and reassuring. It calmed her and pushed her fear aside. They passed two men with Hoover Movers floating in front of them. "Watch the Hoover Movers," Warren said. "They have eyes."

"What?"

"Their screens can watch you and take a screenshot and then send your facial recognition to their computers." Changing the subject, he asked, "Thirsty?"

"Oh, yes. Very." She hadn't had anything to drink in hours and was touched he'd remembered the reason she'd gone into the lounge in the first place.

He turned her toward a kiosk. She selected a bottle of cranberry juice and he got two bottles of water. "We both need to hydrate," he said.

She eyed a turkey sandwich. "I wonder if their sandwiches are fresh. Are you hungry?"

Just then, the woman in the purple turban walked up beside her and stood looking at the sandwiches.

29

Goodness, she smells, such a strong onion smell. Is it just a coincidence that she's here? Clarissa wondered.

Warren's arm moved around Clarissa's waist and he pulled her closer, drawing her away from the woman. "Let's just get our drinks now, hon. We don't want to be late meeting your aunt and uncle."

Aunt and uncle? My aunt is dead and she never married. Glancing up at Warren and catching his expression, she remembered to pretend. Now, the woman was watching her. "I can wait. It's nice with just the two of us." But she moved with him over to the register to check out.

The checkout girl said, "Sluthe is fifty percent off today when you sign up for the frequent buyer card."

"No thank you," Clarissa said and her tone made the girl lean back a bit.

"Not a fan I take it," Warren said and laughed.

"Not at all."

"Good."

Warren paid for the drinks, and they set off down the terminal toward the entrance. They hurried until they stepped on the moving sidewalk, which was jam-packed with people on the other end.

"Rest here for a moment," he said. "Drink."

They opened their drinks and then stood sipping, as there weren't any other passengers around them at the moment while the sidewalk moved them along at a fast clip. "Once that end clears we'll move quickly," he said.

Clarissa asked quietly, "This new gastrointestinal illness, what is it?"

"They claim it's spread by a new variety of super onions. They were released in supermarkets four weeks ago. You haven't seen them?"

She shook her head. "No, I haven't cooked anything with onions lately. What does 'super onion' mean, exactly?"

"These are bigger white onions, which they claim won't make your eyes water when you cut them, and for half the cost of the common onion."

"Really? Do they taste good?"

"I have no idea. I won't eat that modified garbage they're trying to pass off as food. As soon as the onions hit the market people started getting sick. Every single one had eaten those onions. News spread the story of a new gastrointestinal illness, and of course they said nothing about the onions. If not for the Intel we received, I wouldn't have known either. Two days later, they followed the story up with a report the government had come up with a preventative vaccination named Sendot."

"So that's what the announcement was about."

"Yes." He leaned down to whisper in her ear, and the rumbles of his voice made her want to close her eyes and curl up beside him. "It's a lie, though; Sendot does nothing for that illness."

"That's horrible." She turned to face him. "Why would they lie about that?"

"I'll tell you later."

He kissed her forehead and turned her back around, his hands firm on her arms, but not before she noticed the woman in the purple turban again. She was moving closer to them too. Soon, she'd be close enough for Clarissa to smell her. "Warren?"

Bending to kiss her ear he whispered into it, "I know."

His words and the tone of his voice sent a warm shiver down her ear, warmth tingling in her belly as his voice touched something deep inside of her.

What is it about his voice?

He'd straightened back up. "Watch your step." They'd reached the end of one moving sidewalk and hurried between it and the next one.

Clarissa was relieved she hadn't taken Sendot or eaten onions. Now, if she could just get out of this shuttle terminal.

She could smell the garlic and onion stench, which meant the woman must be right behind them. Clarissa worried the woman had something to do with the super onions, and hugged Warren's arm tighter.

"If you're hungry, there's supposed to be a good Vietnamese place about thirty minutes from here. I know you have allergies and they'll cook the food to order."

Allergies, she thought. *I have food allergies?* She gave him a perplexed look.

"Onions." He spoke the word low then raised his voice again. "You'll love it."

Oh right. The onions. She certainly wasn't going to be eating onions any time soon. Developing a sudden allergy to onions was a very smart thing to do. "That sounds good. I like Vietnamese Pho soup."

A man merged with them before they stepped onto the next moving sidewalk his orange shoes standing out, just like the ones she'd seen before.

"I know you do, sweetheart. I just wasn't sure if you'd want to eat now, or if you wanted to wait for a late dinner with your aunt and uncle."

"What?" She looked up at Warren who was watching the man, while appearing not to.

"Check your phone and see if they've called. It's possible they ate lunch before they flew in."

She pulled out her phone. There were no calls, but she now had phone service. She'd received a text from the shuttle company.

Clarissa Heat, report to the shuttle security office. Your previous ticket is invalid, but we have your new ticket. You must report to the shuttle security office to continue to your destination in the Caribbean.

She looked up at Warren, alarm in her eyes.

He took in her expression and the message on the screen. "Buttercup." He ran his hand across the back of her neck. "If you only knew how much I want to kiss you right now."

Kiss me? Her thoughts were a jumble of bad guys after her and this handsome SEAL who wanted to kiss her. While her body screamed yes, kiss, kiss, kiss, like a chanting stadium, her mind said, are you crazy? You can't be kissing here and now when bad guys are after you.

"On second thought." Warren's voice made her focus on him as he spoke, and she looked into his eyes. "Forget about calling them. Let's hurry. I can't wait to get you alone." They stepped off the moving sidewalk and turned right, picking up the pace.

The man in the orange shoes turned right as they did. Now Clarissa was certain he was the same man who'd walked past her by the trashcan. "Warren?"

"Yes, love?"

"I really need to tell you something privately."

"We don't have time, love."

The way the endearment rolled off his tongue made her toes want to curl, an incongruous feeling with her building fear.

The man in the orange shoes and the woman in the purple turban were following and watching her. She wasn't crazy. She'd felt something odd about them when she'd first entered the shuttle station. Her intuition had been trying to tell her something, and right now, it was screaming. The hairs on the back of her neck stood on end and she was in full alert.

Feeling in danger felt much different than being told she was in danger, and she could no longer hide the fear crawling up her spine...

How can Warren remain so calm?

With his arm around her waist, he moved her near a trashcan and dropped his half-empty water bottle in. The man with the orange shoes and the woman in the purple turban moved past them as Warren bent to kiss her ear. "Now. Tell me fast."

"Those two people are following me."

"Yes, I know."

"You do?"

"Of course."

"The woman in the purple turban is the one who bumped into me earlier—she reeks of garlic and onions—and that man wearing orange tennis shoes was there too."

"I'm going to kiss you now, really kiss you."

He bent her back, dipping her into a kiss, her head cradled in the bent elbow of his arm. Her arms came up around his shoulders to hold on, his lips quickly descending to meet hers. Instantly the warm and tender touch of his lips pulled everything inside of her to want more. More taste, more touch, more everything. Her senses came alive in one huge yes, and her mouth opened to him. His tongue touched hers, leaving her senses reeling.

When he let her up, she wanted him to pull her back down to do it again. It was the best and the deepest first kiss she'd ever received and it was over much too fast.

"You're right, baby. So right for me." His words were jarring coming upon the end of such a kiss, but his hand moved down to grasp hers and he gave her a squeeze, as if he knew she was feeling shaken and their kiss deserved a better follow up. "I just hope you can put up with and keep up with me."

As he spoke, she realized he constantly scanned everything around them, like a SEAL would do, which was good, as he'd left her completely twitter pated. Had they been in an old Disney film, birds would've been chirping. But they didn't have time for that, not with those people after her and so many people in the airport to watch and listen.

How did he manage to kiss her like that and still keep up with everything around them? Wasn't he as affected by the kiss as she was?

"Let's go." Warren moved faster and she had to quicken her steps to keep up with him as he pushed to get closer to the exit. Near the exit, Clarissa saw the man in the orange shoes had stopped to buy a newspaper and was watching them. The back of her neck tingled and fear rose in her chest again, breath quickening and stomach churning.

"Time to find our taxi. I can't wait to get you alone," Warren said.

His words made her focus on him again and she blushed. "I want that too," she whispered. Her heart now racing from excitement as much as fear, her body reacting to Warren, her thoughts momentarily turned to what they might do alone.

After they passed the man in the orange shoes, his voice dropped low. "We won't talk anymore, understand?"

She nodded, wanting nothing more than for Warren to get her out of the airport. Now.

"Good. I'm going to kiss you again, and then we'll hold hands and run for that taxi."

"Yes." She'd barely breathed the words before his lips touched hers again. He kissed her so passionately that when he broke away, her only thoughts were to run for that taxi and hurry to get in bed, something her body very much wanted right now. Fear said run, lust said touch me, hold me, have sex now, and her body was in full response mode from his kisses.

They walked quickly past one of the security

checkpoints, and as the guards watched them, he checked his watch. "We're going to be late. Come on."

"I'm trying. Your legs are longer." It was true, he left her winded. *Or is that the kissing?*

As they headed for the sliding glass doors that led outside the shuttle station, a man behind them shouted, "Clarissa! Clarissa Heat!"

She wished she could fly and launch them both into one of those hovering taxis to race far away to safety. *Almost there.*

Just then, a short, bald man stepped in front of them, holding a notepad. "Clarissa Heat? The belly dancer?" She paused automatically, giving herself away. "Please, can you sign something for me? I saw you dancing at the Harem Lounge in Memphis."

"Sorry, she doesn't have time, we're late." Warren pulled her away to the curb where five taxis hovered above the taxi stand, their lights blinking as they waited to be called down for a passenger.

The diesel exhaust fumes filling the air overhead made her eyes water and she blinked fast, glad Warren was holding her hand and guiding her.

He spoke to the dispatcher at the stand, "We're in a hurry. Downtown dinner engagement."

The dispatcher spoke into his radio and then one of the taxis floated down to the curb near where they stood waiting. The man turned to them. "You'll be in number five."

They hurried over to the taxi and the driver got out and reached for Clarissa's bag. "Where to?"

"I'll tell you once we're in the air." Warren gave him her bag and then he helped her into the taxi, and as she climbed in, she saw the man with the orange shoes talking to the dispatcher at the taxi stand. Warren climbed in after her, closed the door, and pulled off his backpack, which he placed on the floor.

When the man with the notepad knocked on the window, she jumped. "Please, Miss Heat, one autograph, please."

Warren shook his head and leaned toward the taxi driver, who'd gotten in and closed his door. "Take us to Perimeter Mall. Fifty-dollar tip if we're not late to meet our friends."

Now the woman in the purple turban was talking to the man in the orange shoes and pointing toward the taxi as it rose into the air.

Warren pulled Clarissa close, kissing her forehead. "Breathe, sweetheart."

She took a breath, not realizing she'd been holding onto so much tension. Leaning against him, she felt safe enclosed in his warm, strong arms. "I'm glad we got away."

The taxi driver watched them in his rear-view mirror as the rest of her words were cut off with a sudden kiss that took her breath away. As intense as the first kiss, her body responded even more. The first had set a wave of craving in motion, and now they were in the taxi, a more private setting, Warren indulged the time they had. His tongue touched hers and hers met his in a dance. They playfully each tried and tasted each other. When she relaxed fully into the fun, sensually delighting in that playfulness, he deepened the kiss. A deeper kiss, more of a yes, I want to take your clothes off kind, which made every thought Clarissa had flee.

Breaking away, Warren let her come up for air

She hadn't been kissed this much in the entire first year of her marriage. Long, lingering kisses were nothing like what she was used to. Deep, playful kisses followed by the intense I want you naked now kind, were a new experience for her. The men she'd been with had liked watching her belly dance, and they'd been more of the watching type. Mostly they'd just wanted to get her into bed for fast and visual sex. There was no time for long make out sessions full of kissing. There was only a quick kiss or two if it seemed obligatory. Joe always made a big deal about how much he liked to watch her. He'd even put mirrors on the ceiling after they were married. "Do this angle now, baby," he'd say. Everything had become a performance. Funny how though belly dancers never stripped, he'd insisted she do that for him at home. Every time. And she had, until she'd realized he'd wanted more. He'd wanted his own harem. And he'd wanted to videotape her. He really wasn't interested in watching her dance, though he'd faked it at first. Once he got her doing strip teases for him at home he'd never gone to see any of her public belly dance gigs. Not one. Thank God she was done stripping for him. He wouldn't take one more thing away from her.

She shouldn't compare the two men, for there was no comparison. Though she couldn't help it at first, they were so different. Warren was like no man she'd ever met before.

Warren's kisses made her close her eyes and forget where she was or what she looked like. They were like her favorite dessert; she couldn't turn it down or get enough. If a man who could kiss her the way Warren did ever stopped after she'd gotten used to it, that would be a sort of death.

Where is this going? It will end once I'm safe, he'll walk away. The thought made her stomach hurt, and scenery flew by as she stared out the window, lost in her thoughts with her fingertips to her lips.

Warren watched her with light in his deep brown eyes. "Daydreaming?"

Blushing, she dropped her hand into her lap. Did he know what his kisses did to her? She wondered how many women he'd kissed to be so very good at it. He was the best kisser she'd ever met. She wondered if he could read her or if she was just that obvious to him. By the grin on his face and the look in his eyes, he knew the effect his kisses had on her.

He reached over and threaded his fingers through hers, warm and strong. She gave him a shy smile.

"Let's talk about your fans. Does that happen often?"

"Does what happen? Them wanting my autograph?" She shrugged. "Usually, after a show, they do."

"Let me guess, first they want your autograph on the program, and then they want to buy you a drink, while hoping for something more."

His eyes seemed wise as he spoke, but her defenses went up immediately.

"Before you get the wrong idea, belly dancers are not strippers. I never drink when I'm in costume, I don't perform at bachelor parties or all-male events, and I don't do belly grams. I always have an escort, and I do not sleep around."

He gave a nod and paused before speaking. "How well-known are you?"

"I didn't think I was, outside of the belly dance community in Memphis. Photographers tend to follow me, they all want pictures."

"So, was that man the first time someone came up to you, apart from the shows?"

Clarissa nodded.

"Interesting."

What does he really think? How will I ever know if all he ever says is interesting?

He pulled her close and said, "That would take some getting used to. I'm not sure I'd like men approaching my girl that way." He ran his finger across her cheek and jaw. "I'd want you all to myself."

She caught the taxi driver watching them again and realized Warren was putting on a show for him. He kissed her again, then, and there was no pretense in it—she could've sworn to it, though this third kiss was brief. When she closed her eyes, she could've sworn this was real, not pretend. *Or is it? Maybe I'm not so good at telling what's real. My ex-husband had me fooled.*

"We're almost there."

She wished they weren't and that he'd kiss her again. *Now he'll say goodbye and I'll never see him again. Three times is a charm, right? Three and then we're done. This last kiss is short. Maybe that's his way of ending it. And now, here we are. Too soon, they were floating down in front of the mall, getting out of the taxi.*

Warren paid the driver and picked up her bag. "Let's go inside and look at a few shop windows on the way." He took her hand as the taxi drove off. "You're stuck with me a while longer."

41

Stuck? "I like being stuck with you."

"Good. I was thinking you'd be ready for this to all be over." He smiled at her as they walked toward the mall entrance.

"Well, this is the part I like, being with you. Not the other part."

"If you liked the other part, I'd be very concerned."

"No one could like that."

"You'd be surprised. I've met a few who get off on danger."

"That's crazy."

"No, not crazy. It's the adrenaline rush. It ramps up your sexual drive and in some people their emotions."

Oh…so that explains it. Maybe I'm not falling in love; there's no love at first sight, and this is just adrenaline and danger making me feel this way.

"Those two were following you, and so was the man with the notepad."

"I thought he just wanted an autograph?"

"Clarissa, you're a beautiful woman and I'm sure you're a great dancer, but you're not famous enough for that. Think about it, you're a long way from Memphis."

"You're right. It was a weird thing to happen. I'm a belly dancer, not a famous rock star."

"They'll know where we've gone and may send a team after us. So, we're going to walk around this mall, let people see us, and then we're going to exit. We'll walk to the bus stop and take the bus to where my friend has a Harley I can borrow."

"A motorcycle?"

"Yes."

She blinked twice as she took in the information. "But only people in that patriot rebel group ride motorcycles on the ground...or gang members. Everyone else rides the shuttles or flying taxis and flying passenger vans."

"Yes."

Warren was getting more interesting the more she got to know him. *Was he in that rebel group or in a gang?* It was more dangerous to drive anything on the ground. Ten or twelve car jacking's a week were the norm before more people took to commuting together in the flying air buses. Now it was mostly those who couldn't afford the van rides or who didn't want to, for whatever reason, that drove cars or rode bikes or walked. But a motorcycle? *Wow. Only tough guys did that.* "How do your motorcycles avoid being picked up by the federal police vans from the air?"

"Harleys have a certain vibration which can be modified to avoid detection. You'd know it if you'd ever been near one. Can't mistake that rumble. There's an instrument we've attached to the bike that, along with the vibration, jams them from below. What shows up on their system looks like a big truck, instead. And not one of them have figured that out yet."

"Wow. There are so many trucks on the highways. I bet you guys blend right in."

"From the air, we do. It'll only work until they finish the new flying police cars. They'll be able to fly lower and hover close within eyesight." Warren bent his head to look up bus schedules on his phone and she thought about the new cars. It was bad enough with the shuttles flying up high and the helicopters and vans and now flying cars. All that busyness in the air in the cities and the militia everywhere made traveling anywhere stressful for Clarissa. Those vans would land and militia teams would come pouring out.

She studied Warren's profile. Missing her flight had been the best thing that could've happened to her. Warren was handsome, brave, and looking out for her. This was the kind of experience so many girls dreamed of, and why they read so many romance novels. *Here I am, getting to live that dream. The kissing alone is worth missing my vacation. I wish he'd kiss me again. I wish I wasn't on the run and we had more time.*

"Okay, in about fifteen minutes we'll leave and get on the bus. Once we're on the Harley and far away, we'll find a place to talk—really talk."

"I've been okay with not talking." She couldn't believe she was bold enough to say that. With the kissing, however, they'd already crossed the line from strangers to feeling like she knew him somehow. "I'd be okay with not talking again."

He smiled at the light in her eyes and pulled her toward him. "That could be arranged."

"I'd like that," she said.

He pulled her closer and brought his fingertips up to caress her cheek. She smiled, leaning into his hand, and he bent down and kissed her. It was soft at first this time, and her eyes drifted closed as one of his hands slid behind her neck, beneath her hair. His other moved to her lower back, pulling her against him. He held her as the passion of their kiss arose the passion within her,

44

sweeping her into a cloud of sensations.

She opened her mouth to him, deepening and intensifying the kiss, as he guided her toward the wall with both of his arms now around her waist. He moved her back until she was pressed against the wall, his commanding manner made her weak in the knees as she relaxed. His taller, broader body sheltered her from anyone's view, and she forgot to worry about what someone might see or think. He was muscular and strong and as he pressed against her further, she realized how much he wanted her, everything in his kiss pulling her to want him too.

Caught up in the kiss, there was only him; his touch, his taste, his scent, his breath, his tongue, and his hard length against her, telling her how much he desired her. She would've stayed this way forever, following wherever this took them. Suddenly, he stopped.

CHAPTER FOUR

Her eyes flew open. *Why did he stop?*
Disappointment filled her and she craved his return.
Desire ran rampant through her body, every inch of her
alive. *His kiss was so amazing.* She wanted more.

"We have to go. Now."

"What?"

He took her by the hand, pulling her along as he
strode toward the exit. "Trust me."

"I'm trying to." She hurried along beside him.
Crazy as it was, she did trust him. Everything about him
told her she could, and she needed to trust him to be
safe. Doubts and insecurities had no place here and
now.

Once he'd pulled her outside the mall, he spoke
quickly, "The man with the orange shoes is here."

"Oh my God. He followed us?" She turned to look
over her shoulder, but Warren pulled her hand,
redirecting the angle of her body toward him.

"Yes," his voice was urgent. "But he ditched the
shoes. Let's go."

They hurried across the street with Warren still
holding her hand. Shuttles, vans and taxis moved about
in the sky above them and two trucks came down the

street just as they passed, their diesel fuel making the air stink. The only pedestrians were headed toward the bus station. It wasn't safe to walk very far on the streets. Anyone who had money to afford it took to the air for transport, which left the poor, and the criminals who preyed on them, the run of the streets. On her own, to insure her safety, Clarissa would've called for a taxi to go where she wanted to go. But with Warren, things were different.

She liked how he took charge. It made her feel safe, even in the midst of being pursued. There was just something about him. The bus floated down one minute after they reached the bus stop. "You timed that well," she said.

"The bus was right on schedule." He nodded and continued to scan the area as they boarded.

Slipping into a seat at the back of the bus, Warren kissed her ear again after they sat. When the bus rose into the air he whispered into her ear, "Cameras aboard. Let's make out."

She nodded as his words made her tingle with anticipation. Her stomach flipped as the bus lifted into the air and flew forward. He kissed her ear. She gave a slight shiver and wanted more. She needed to feel alive, needed to stay alive.

He pulled her onto his lap and turned her to face him before kissing her neck.

She felt people watching, but no one commented, and her hair now formed a curtain around them.

"Would you be interested in more than making out?" he whispered in her ear.

"Mmm hmm," she hummed, feeling his lips smile

against her neck.

"Good." His tone made her smile. *Yes, this is very good.*

Clarissa closed her eyes and let him kiss her as her hand drifted down to rest upon his very hard abs. She imagined what it would feel like to ride behind him on that motorcycle, holding onto him. She imagined what it would feel like to ride him.

As he kissed her, all thoughts drifted away, leaving only the urge to hike up her sundress, and let her panties fall, following the need to touch him and to be touched.

He caressed her breast, her nipple responded and she shifted on his lap. She wanted to rub up against him and find release. She wanted fulfillment. She reached toward her panties—the dress would cover everything—but Warren pulled away.

He brushed back her hair with a gentle hand and smiled. "We'll be getting off soon."

She blinked, catching her breath, and it took a moment for the reality of what he'd said to register. *Off the bus. He meant off the bus.* My God, people were after her and all she could think of was getting naked with Warren. She was out of control and she needed to get it back.

She sat up and slid back onto her seat, her face heated. She avoided looking at the other passengers. *I'll be a pool of melted butter by the time we get where we're going if this keeps up.* She didn't know which was more dangerous; the people who were after her, or forgetting about them with Warren. Clarissa caught herself then. Both were dangerous, she needed to stop letting Warren kiss her. Somehow, when he did, she lost the ability to think. She needed to be sure she was safe and far away from the people chasing her before she could think about taking things further with the man next to her. And who was chasing her? And why? She needed answers. Just as she was about to ask him, he pulled her from her thoughts.

"Anything in your bag you can't live without?"

"Yes. Why?"

"We need to leave your carry-on and get off this bus as fast as we can."

Frowning, she got out her jeans and pulled them up beneath her dress, the opposite of what she'd wanted to do just minutes ago, when she'd wanted to pull both their clothes off. What had she been thinking? This man made her lose all sense. People were chasing her and she was acting like a horny teenager.

"Can I tuck the dress in and make it look more like a top? I'm going to look funny like this."

"The yellow is noticeable."

The reminder she was still being pursued chased away her amorous mood and she frowned at him. "Well I'm not getting undressed on a bus."

She switched her sandals for socks and tennis shoes, and pulled her lucky coin belt out, wrapping it around her waist.

"You'll have to leave that behind. It makes too much noise and it's too eye-catching."

Red fabric with four layers of gold coins was, in fact, quite noticeable, which was perfect on stage beneath the lights as she danced and shimmied.

"I need my belt, I'm not leaving without it." She

49

tugged her sundress over it, which would hide the colors, but only mute the noise.

No way was she leaving her lucky coin belt, especially not when she couldn't think straight around him.

"See? Hidden."

"But not silent." He shook his head and frowned.

Stubborn, she crossed her arms. "I'm not leaving it."

The bus glided down to a stop and the doors opened.

"No time to argue," he said. "We've got to go."

When they stood, Warren tickled her, surprising her. She squealed and he chased her down the aisle, making her giggle as they made their way to the front of the bus. The other passengers watched them, and Clarissa blushed as she jingled down the aisle.

Once off the bus, he took her hand in a firm, reassuring grip and walked briskly down the sidewalk.

"You're a tickle monster," she said with a laugh.

"I had to do something to distract them from your coin belt and try to make more noise than it did. You're very ticklish."

"Yes, I am. But I liked it." She laughed and he sent her a grin.

The sun had already gone down, and when they rounded the corner into the residential section, the stars were out. Shadows had begun to creep across the lawns. They moved slowly with him putting an arm across her shoulders, and moving her into the shadows, if he thought he heard or saw anyone coming. Good people did not roam the streets at night, which meant anyone they ran into was likely to be a potential problem.

"You're very cautious, but I like it. It makes me feel safe." She spoke quietly, calmer now.

"I'm not taking chances. You're in my care." His tone and his words reassured her, making her feel even safer.

He led her to a dark spot behind a house, and then he reached into his backpack. "Now you can ditch the dress." He pulled out a navy-blue T-shirt with a gold trident screen-printed on the right chest. "Here."

She took the T-shirt, turned her back to him, and pulled off the sundress. Aware that he could see her bare back and the crescent moon tattooed on her left shoulder, she quickly put on the shirt and readjusted the belt around her hips.

"The coin belt needs to go too."

"No," she spoke sharply into the night air, grateful he hadn't asked about the tattoo. That story would have to wait. His command to leave the coin belt didn't sit well with her, but she'd come out sounding testier than she'd meant to. All the stress of the day had poured into that word, and he'd immediately gone silent. He was so silent it made her nervous, because she didn't know what he was thinking, and it reminded her she didn't know him very well.

"Ready?" His voice sounded strained.

"Ready." She handed him the dress, which he wadded up and dropped into a nearby trashcan. "Hey, I liked that dress!"

"They've seen you in it. It wouldn't be wise to wear it again. They're looking for a woman in a yellow dress, not a navy T-shirt and jeans." He gave her a determined look and continued, "They may be looking for that coin belt too. They'll be listening for it. You'll attract too much attention instead of blending in."

She cut him off. "I still wish I could've kept that dress. I never got to wear it, but this once."

He took hold of her hand and squeezed. "Sweetheart, once you're safe, I'll buy you a new dress. You should ditch the coin belt, though, lucky or not. It won't be lucky if they catch you because of it."

"I'm not leaving it. This belt has always brought me good luck, and I need all the luck I can get right now."

"You're nuts." He shook his head, frustration clear. "Come on, then." He looked up and down the alley, scanning as he spoke. "I need to get you inside. We'll move slowly." Exasperated he looked at her. "Try not to jingle."

They moved through the shadows, dodging lights and any people. Finally, they reached a small, brick house. He led her to the back door and knocked.

An older man with greying hair and tattoos covering his arms opened the door. "Damn. Didn't expect to see you tonight."

"Do you ever expect me?"

"No." Pete laughed. "You turn up at the damnedest times. Come on in."

They followed him in and waited while he closed, locked, and dead-bolted the door.

"Pete, this is Clarissa. She's in a bit of trouble." The two men exchanged a look, and then Warren turned to her. "Clarissa, Pete and I served together. You can trust him."

Pete shook her hand, and she noted his strength. This was no regular older man; this man worked out, worked hard or both. She smiled. "Nice to meet you, Pete."

"Likewise, Clarissa." He gave her the once-over, noting her coin belt. "Now, who's bothering a pretty little thing like you?" He cracked his knuckles. "Boyfriend? Husband? Ex? We'll see he behaves more respectfully. We can also make him go away."

"No. There's no man to make go away."

"Well, then sit down, make yourselves comfortable, and tell me about it." He gestured to the living room.

They moved out of the kitchen and sat, Warren slid his arm around her. She scooted closer and relaxed against him. "Clarissa was in the shuttle station in that lounge that got busted up. I found her sleeping there when I went to check it out."

"Did you, now?" Pete's eyes were merry. "I've got to tell you, lass, this one has a way of finding pretty damsels in distress."

Warren gave a sigh of exasperation, and Clarissa watched him with curiosity. *He didn't like his buddy telling me that.*

"Did they inject her?" Pete had gone from teasing to serious as he directed the question to his friend.

"No. I found her just before, and we've been

dodging them since."

Pete nodded. "You'll want one of my Harleys. The black one's got just over half a tank. Do you need money?"

"No, I've got that covered."

She cocked her head. "How did you know about the lounge? What happened in there?"

He watched her for a moment and took his time answering. "Warren and I...we keep an eye on things."

"I see. Why was the lounge trashed?"

"The first day they started injecting Sendot into passengers, they got hold of two active duty Marines who didn't take too kindly to it. The fight moved to that lounge," Pete said.

"It's a good thing you didn't touch that white foam" Warren said. "It's called Rida and it causes chemical burns if it touches your skin. Several airport employees went to the hospital with chemical burns. Even spraying the foam, they still couldn't capture and detain the Marines. Once away, they alerted our special forces community about what was happening with the forced injections."

"They're forcing people?"

"Yes, ma'am. Some folks are real determined to get anyone flying out of the country chipped and tagged."

"Chipped and..." Her jaw dropped open and she squeaked as her voice rose in pitch. "They were going to plant a chip in me?"

Warren, who'd been silent, squeezed her shoulder. "You're safe now."

"That's what Sendot is," Pete said. "A tiny little chip you'd hardly notice. From then on, they'd be tracking you. What's even worse is they're telling everyone this shot has to be taken in the stomach. It's painful and unnecessary."

"Why would anyone allow that?"

"Because they think they'll die from that gastro disease if they don't," Warren said.

Clarissa's eyes widened and she looked back and forth between them in horror. "People who think they can't get that intestinal illness might catch it anyway and die?"

"Correct." Pete nodded. "The one way to avoid their so-called illness is to avoid eating those onions, that's what's spreading it. Our team has developed a sudden allergy to onions, and I suggest you do the same."

"Onions. That's crazy." This whole thing seemed unreal. She was having trouble soaking it in. "So…they created the problem just so they could fake fix it?"

"Now you're catching on." Pete winked. "We don't know of a cure for the illness."

Clarissa shook her head with a frown. "Onions are in so many things. It won't be easy to avoid them."

"No, it won't," Pete agreed. "That's why you tell people you're allergic."

"So," Warren paused, waiting for her full attention. "you do know you can't go back to your place, right? They'll be watching it."

"But I—where will I go?" She frowned. "What

about my things? I don't even have a change of clothes now."

"You've still got your purse, everything important should be in there. Things can be bought. Your life is more precious than things. We can replace everything else." His gaze went to her hips.

"Like my coin belt?" Her hand moved to it, as if he'd try to take it. "No, I won't give it up."

Pete cleared his throat and they both looked at him. "Those two marines, they disappeared two days ago and no one has heard from them since. They'd both gone home on leave."

"Oh." Clarissa gasped, her hands flying to her mouth. Whispering into her hands, she said, "They killed them."

"Maybe. Maybe not." Warren squeezed her shoulder. "It's not easy to kill a Marine. We'll keep you safe. You'll stay with me, but you need to do as I say."

Eyes wide, she looked up at him. The voice of command was strong in him and every part of her wanted to follow. As much as his voice pulled at her, though, she hesitated.

"If that meets your approval." Warren watched for her reaction. "If not, Pete will find you one of our other members. Whatever you decide, you must not go home again."

Never go home again? Never collect my things? A tear rolled down her face. Would she be on the run or in hiding forever? Caught up in her thoughts and emotions, she didn't speak. Both men remained silent, waiting for her answer, and Warren rubbed her shoulder to comfort her.

Finally, she whispered, "I'm scared."

"Scared to leave your home, or scared to be with me?"

"Oh." She turned to face him fully. "I'm not scared of you, you've made me feel safe. It's just…this is a lot to ask. I haven't even known you for twenty-four hours, yet, I'm supposed to go off with you and never go home again? That's a lot to ask."

"You need to make a decision quickly and then get on the road." Pete stood. "When did you two last eat?"

Clarissa's stomach was rumbling loudly enough for everyone to hear it. "Breakfast," she said.

"I bet you ate one of those watch-your-figure breakfasts."

"Yes." She smiled at him. "Toast and tea. How did you guess?"

"Dancers," he said. "I've had some experience. Don't know how you keep them curves, on toast and tea." He snorted, shaking his head. "I'll make you both sandwiches. Ham and cheese is all this old bachelor has to offer tonight."

"That sounds good," Cyree said. "Thank you, Pete."

"You're welcome darlin'." Pete headed for the kitchen.

Warren reached for her hand, brought it to his lips and kissed it, then gave it a squeeze. "Follow what I tell you for your safety when I give an order, but the decisions for everything else are yours. Agreed?"

That isn't so bad. She watched him, thinking how

easy he was making this difficult thing for her. "Yes, I can agree to that."

When she asked where the bathroom was, Pete popped his head around the corner from the kitchen. "Straight down the hall and to the left. Help yourself to whatever you need, but keep in mind you don't have time for a long shower or girly primping."

Clarissa headed toward the bathroom.

"Oh, and Clarissa?" Warren spoke again. She turned to look at him. "Lose the coin belt."

"No, I—"

He cut her off. "At least take it off and stow it in a bag. It's too damn…"

"Too damn what?" Her hands went to her hips and she glared at him.

"Never mind." He threw up his hand and headed for the garage door, grumbling. "That woman and her hips…"

"Mighty distracting, aren't they?" Pete interrupted from the kitchen, laughter in his voice. Warren's response was to slam the garage door, which made Pete laugh.

Clarissa giggled to herself as she went into the bathroom. She did the necessaries and walked back into the living room, where the men and her sandwich were now waiting. She smiled at Warren and held the hip scarf in her hand. "No more jingling. I'm keeping it close, though. It brings me good luck."

A memory flashed through her mind and her thoughts drifted.

The belt held happy memories. If she had to leave everything behind, she was glad she had it to remind her.

"Compromise can be a good thing," Pete said. "You kids remember that. In a good relationship, it can be essential. That'll be fifty cents, and be sure to send me a wedding invitation."

"All right, you old fart." Warren was ready to say something else when Clarissa spoke.

"Now, let me get this straight. They created a food that makes everyone sick, and instead of taking it off the grocery store shelves, they're handing out Sendot, which doesn't cure the illness."

"Correct," Warren said.

She closed her eyes, took a breath, let it out, and looked at Warren again. "I feel like my whole world has just shifted."

He pulled her close. "That's because it has."

"Why were you in that lounge?"

"We needed to plant a bug—I volunteered."

She smiled. "I'm glad you volunteered, and I'm glad I didn't get on that shuttle."

"Where were you headed on the shuttle?" Pete asked.

"Grand Cayman. I was overdue for a vacation. I just went through a divorce and wanted to get away."

"Divorce is rough. Been through one of those myself during my first tour. It gets easier," Warren said.

"Mine was pretty bad. My husband was having an affair with my attorney and I didn't find out until right before the final settlement. Joe was no good. He slept with half the women I knew and tried to take my house and all of my inheritance."

He gave her a quick hug. "I'm glad you're free now."

"Me too."

When he released her, he pointed to a plate on the table. "Now eat, we need to get on the road."

Pete handed Warren the keys to his bike and addressed Clarissa as she took the first bite of her sandwich. "Sounds like a bad divorce. Let him have the house, he's going to have a hell of a time when they start in on him, wanting to know where you've gone. Of course, I could rough him up for you, or even make him disappear..."

"Oh no, that would be extreme and I don't want them coming after you. I've got to let all that go. I need to move into the future, but I've been having a little trouble with it."

"Well, darlin', if you go racing off with Warren on that Harley, I'd say you'll have a great start with a good future ahead of you. This time with a real man, instead of some asswipe who won't treat you right."

Warren, who'd been watching her in silence as he listened said, "A change of scenery will be good for you."

Her eyes lit up. "That's just what I've been saying I needed! It's like you can read my mind."

"No, I can't read your mind. I just pay attention."

"Warren's real good at reading people," Pete said.

"It's nothing special." Warren shrugged.

"Most men don't pay attention," Clarissa said.

"Most men aren't Navy SEALs," Pete said. "We're unique, and Warren is one of the best."

She touched his arm and said, "What happened with your first wife?"

"I came back from a deployment to find she'd cleaned out the bank accounts and the house. Emptiest damn house I've ever seen. I did another tour and started over. Life after divorce gets better with time." He nudged her. "You're not eating."

"I was trying to start over, but I didn't plan for all of this. It feels like I've stepped into a cloak and dagger movie." She shook her head. "It's not like I thought it would be at all."

He gave her and the sandwich a stern look and she took another bite, before he asked, "What do you mean?"

She chewed and swallowed. "In the movies, where everyone is a suspect and bad guys jump out of the bushes, it seems exciting. In reality, it's scary and hard to know who the bad guys are, because they look like everyone else. If that guy hadn't had orange shoes, I wouldn't have noticed him, same with the woman in the purple turban."

"They blend in, that's their job," Warren said. "And those things can be ditched in the trash. You won't remember the color of their hair or their height. That's why they wear those attention-getting things; the average person won't look past them."

"You do."

"I've been trained."

She frowned as the thought they might've been watching her before all of this came to her and that something horrible could've happened to her before Warren found her.

They could be watching everywhere and she'd never know. She didn't have the training Warren had. They could've been watching her for months. The thought gave her goose bumps and made her stomach flip. She set her sandwich down, suddenly not hungry anymore. *How long have they been watching me?*

She turned her worried gaze to Warren "How would I know if someone has been watching me? I mean before this happened at the shuttle station?"

"Do you have reason to believe someone was watching you before today?"

Uncertainty and fear filled her. "I don't know, but if they go to my house…"

Warren's eyes searched hers. "What would they find if they searched your house, Clarissa?"

CHAPTER FIVE

"They'll find everything."

"Everything?" Warren took her hands in his. "What would that be?"

"My…my grow room with my herb garden." She gasped. "And all my seeds. I mean all of them! I have jars and jars of seeds. My aunt Lyndsay had a farm and she harvested and sold them. Before it was illegal. I have enough seeds to fill the back of a van. If they find them, they'll think I'm a dealer and they'll send me to prison."

"Where is your grow room, Clarissa?" Pete asked.

"In my spare bedroom. I have a hydroponic garden. The herbs are just for medicinal use, just for me. My aunt gave me the seeds before she passed."

"Before they outlawed the use of herbs for medicinal purposes?" Pete seemed concerned.

"No, after."

"So, you knew growing was against the law." Pete nodded. "You knew the risks."

"It shouldn't be."

"No, it shouldn't," he agreed.

"But yes, I know they'll arrest me if they find out."

DEBRA PARMLEY

"Did your aunt ever have trouble with the authorities?"

"No, at least, never around me."

"Let's hope you haven't done enough to trigger their investigators."

"I don't think I did, but I got the feeling of being watched in the shuttle station."

"She attracted their attention and was being watched," Warren said. "They'll be digging to find out who she is and may be headed to her house already."

"I hope not! All my family heirloom seeds are there! My aunt wanted me to have enough of each type of seed to pass down through the family, if I ever had children. It's supposed to remain a family secret." She looked back and forth between the two men, her eyes wide. "Please, you mustn't tell anyone."

"We're good at keeping secrets, Clarissa," Warren spoke and gave her hands a squeeze of reassurance.

Pete spoke, "You'd be surprised at how many secrets this man has kept." He nodded toward Warren.

"It's part of the job. Men who can't keep a secret don't make it as a SEAL." He spoke as a matter of fact, like it was nothing out of the ordinary. "What about your ex? Does he know about the seeds?"

"Yes, of course. We lived together in that house."

"I'm surprised he didn't turn you in during the divorce. Though if he had, they'd have seized both of you and then seized your house and your seeds."

"He wouldn't be that stupid. Joe always looks out for number one, and Joe is always number one.

64

Everyone else comes second."

Warren and Pete shared a look.

"How many seeds are we talking about?" Pete asked. "You said enough to fill a van. It could be tough, but maybe they can be extracted before they're discovered, if they haven't been already."

"There are rows of metal shelves and those are full, stacked with mason jars and each one is full of a different type of seed."

"Those are valuable. And they'd like nothing more than to destroy them," Pete said. "We've got to get to those seeds first. I'll put a team on that right away. Don't worry about those seeds. We'll take care of that and you. We'll make sure you're safe. Now you need to get on down the road to a safer place where they aren't looking for you."

"Are you sure you aren't on a list already? How do you hide the electricity?" Warren's question brought her attention back to him. "How have you kept your grow room hidden?"

"I have black-out curtains, and I only run the grow lights during the day and use a solar panel on the roof. I haven't told anyone."

"Won't matter, girlie." Pete laughed. "They'll have pegged you as a terrorist for sure, just for having the seeds, even if you never planted one. They're a better treasure than gold. A lot of people would love to get their hands on them."

Worry filled her brow. "They take people away. And those people never come back. My aunt had a book written by an herbalist many years ago and when my aunt bought the copy, the man who sold it to her said never publish one of those books because it would be a death sentence. I asked her about it later and she said there was a quiet war between good men and the men who wanted to kill the knowledge. I was young and didn't understand her then. But she hid the book away and I never did find it. She said it wasn't safe to let anyone see it." Panic filled her. "Now those people are after me. What will they do if they find me?"

"They're not going to find you." Each word was firm as Warren looked into her eyes, his intense gaze telling her he'd do everything in his power to prevent that from happening.

She nodded.

"I know you're in shock, but you'll feel much better after a good night's sleep. We'll drive south and get a room in a town where no one has ever seen you before, where no one knows who you are. Okay?" He leaned in and gave her a quick kiss on the lips before taking the keys from Pete. She nodded and forced her panic back down.

Being near Warren had a calming influence on her. He was solid, strong and capable.

Before you go, I have something for you." Pete gestured for them to follow him and headed for one of the bedrooms, which had been turned into a library. They followed him in and he stopped by a table in the center of the room. "I just need to remember where I put it." He rubbed his chin for a minute and then headed for one of the bookshelves and reached for a tube. Pulling the tube down, he took the cap off the end and looked inside. "Good. It's still there."

Clarissa, distracted by the books on the shelves, wished she could have stayed here for several hours to look around. So many old books, leather bound and those wrapped in cloth, were intriguing. She'd never seen this many real books outside of an antique book store. But they had no time and whatever Pete had in that tube intrigued her as well.

Pete pulled a rolled up paper out of the tube.

"I should've guessed you'd have a map." Warren laughed.

"Of course," Pete said, as if it were the most natural thing in the world to own one. As if maps were still printed even with everyone using GPS systems instead. He rolled the map out on the table and they all leaned over the table to look down at it.

"It's unusually clear," Clarissa said.

"There's been no daylight on it to fade it," Pete said.

"A map in this kind of shape must have been expensive," Clarissa said.

"It would have been had I bought it."

"You stole it?" Clarissa said.

"No. It was more," Pete paused, "you might say a trade."

"Pete has done favors for powerful people," Warren said.

"Jobs." Pete corrected and shook his head. "Not favors." He folded the map and handed it to Warren.

"Thanks," Warren said. "I appreciate this."

"You know I got your six," Pete said.

"Always," Warren said. "And I yours."

Pete nodded and then turned toward the door. "Come on."

They followed Pete into the garage. Three Harleys were stored there, one black, one red and one blue. They looked like the motorcycles with shiny chrome she'd seen in old movies. The ones where there weren't any flying cars or zooming shuttles overhead. Briefly, she wondered what it was like to look up and see only a sky full of clouds. Was it quieter? Like it had been on her aunt's farm? She'd been in such a hurry to move to the city and to be on her own, she'd never learned to appreciate the farm. Clarissa and her mother had always lived in the city, so that was where she'd longed to be when she was a teenager. But the city she'd moved back to wasn't the home she'd remembered. It would never again feel like home.

Pete walked to the black bike, where he put two fresh sandwiches into the saddlebags along with the one she hadn't finished, and added a couple bottles of water, a nine-millimeter gun and ammo.

Clarissa paused, she'd never been around guns and had never shot one before. It was kind of intimidating being around them. The men were all business now and she hung back.

"I figured you'd need that." Pete closed the saddle bag.

"Thanks, Pete."

"You're welcome, brother." He turned to Clarissa. "Come on girl, don't be shy." He handed Clarissa a helmet as Warren put a helmet on. "These bikes are safe. I work on them myself."

"You do the modifications?"

"Yes, I do everything on these bikes."

"How do you keep them from being spotted from the air?"

"You know all the trucks on the highway use Bio-diesel fuel only?"

She nodded. "Yes. I don't think you can even buy the other fuels anymore."

"That's right," Pete said. "Well now, those trucks on the highway have a particular heat signature. Our motorcycles sound like semi-trucks and the trackers in the sky aren't looking for size. The heat signatures of the motorcycle's engine and the noise and exhaust signatures, that's all they're looking for. This motorcycle add-on works with that to make it appear that the motorcycle is just a small semi-truck. I've made all the modifications myself and they run on the same fuel as the trucks."

"That's fascinating."

"This is one way we keep the men and women of Deep Nest safe. And now that you're with Warren, you'll be safe too. So, don't you worry, gal. The bikes are safe and there's no one who'll take better care of you than Warren. If you ever need anything, come on back here to me."

"Thank you, Pete," she said.

The men clasped hands, and then Warren sat on the bike and Clarissa climbed on back.

"Hang on a second," Pete said. He reached into the back of his Jeep and pulled out a worn, black leather jacket. "Here, girlie, throw that on. It's gonna be chilly for ya."

"Oh, I can't take that."

"It's a spare. Take it."

"Thank you again, Pete." She accepted with a smile and pulled the large jacket on. "You're very generous."

He nodded and then spoke to Warren. "You'll check in?"

"We'll go silent for two days."

"Day three then." He gave another nod.

"Why wait so long?" Clarissa asked.

"Silence gives them nothing to find or trace. There's safety in silence."

"Oh. That makes sense."

Pete raised the garage door and Warren fired up the bike. When the Harley was fired up Clarissa thought maybe it wasn't quieter back in the day when more people rode motorcycles. This bike really rumbled. The modification on the bike was the only non-retro part of it. Everything else about it was like stepping back in time. As she sat on the bike, she started to grin. That rumble was really nice. She had a feeling she was going to love this ride.

Soon, they were roaring down the road. Clarissa raised a hand to wave, but Pete was already closing the garage door.

After trying twice to say something to Warren, she realized the Harley was too noisy for talking, so she contented herself with wrapping her arms around him.

Closing her eyes, she leaned into him and inhaled his scent just before they built up speed. Now, they were racing off into the sunset—well, the sun had already set. They were racing off into something, though; that unknown future, just the two of them.

A change of scenery. She didn't necessarily need it to be the Caribbean, any sandy beach would be good. Maybe it was time to revise her mantra of no men, just sand and beach to "just sand and beach."

She suspected anywhere with Warren was bound to be good, but curious, she shouted as loud as she could, "Where are we going?"

"Florida," he shouted back. "I'm taking you to the beach."

She smiled, gave his waist a squeeze and internally squealed. *Can this get any better?* She smiled deeper. *Why yes, it can.* It wasn't long ago she'd thought things could only get worse, and then they had. Maybe things had to get a whole lot worse before they could get better. *I hope the worst is behind us now.* As they roared off into the dark night, she clung to both him and her positive thoughts.

The highway was windy and full of trucks. Warren rode the bike so close to the truck in front of them that she thought he was going to hit it and screamed, clutching him tighter and ducking her head behind his back.

"You okay back there?" he yelled.

"No! We are too close!"

"Have to be," he yelled back. "We don't want to be seen by the drone overhead."

Glancing up she saw a drone flying over the truck

71

they were following. Scared now, she closed her eyes, as if closing them would make her invisible to the drone. Closing them she wouldn't see how close they were to the truck, but she could smell the fumes. She coughed once and then closed her mouth, swallowed and clung on for dear life. The drone finally moved on.

Once she got used to the way he was driving and how it felt riding and had started to relax, because they'd been riding about an hour and nothing bad had happened, she felt safe riding behind Warren on the bike. Riding the Harley was fun! And it made her feel so alive. Warren moved from behind one truck to behind another so they were never away from a truck, never isolated as a lone vehicle on the highway. Clarissa guessed he was doing that to avoid being detected from the air.

When Warren finally drove into the King's Rest Motel parking lot in Hazlehurst, Georgia, Clarissa was so hungry she felt faint. She wished she'd been able to eat more than a few bites of her sandwich back at Pete's house.

As she got off the Harley, her legs were wobbly and she was sore from four hours on the bike. They'd only stopped once, at an old gas station, after they'd been on the road for two hours and he'd deemed it safe enough to stop, so she could use the not-so-clean restroom with a door that wouldn't lock. Warren had stood in front of it to keep anyone from trying to enter, and they hadn't stayed long. But at least she'd had a break after riding for two hours.

Four hours was a long time when her body wasn't used to riding. That rumble she'd liked so much at first had worn her out. Now dizzy, she swayed.

Warren caught her by the elbow and asked, "Are

you all right?"

"I just need to eat something and lie down."

"As soon as I get us checked in you can do that. I'll get us a room." He unfastened her helmet, took it off, and placed it on the bike. "Why don't you sit on that bench outside the office?"

After guiding her to the metal bench, he hurried inside where the young desk clerk sat behind the counter, her head bobbing in time to music playing on the hoover mover floating beside her. When he came back to Clarissa, she stood and wavered as another wave of dizziness hit.

"I might need to carry you," he said.

"What? I wouldn't want you to pull something."

He scooped her into his arms. "Sweetheart, you're no trouble at all." She smiled and relaxed, thinking she really liked this.

The desk clerk was grinning as she watched from where she stood in the doorway, the hoover mover following her playing techno pop. "Newlyweds," he called to her and winked.

"Congratulations," the girl giggled.

Clarissa giggled too. "She thinks you're carrying me off to our honeymoon."

"I know." As he walked far enough the clerk wouldn't hear him he said, "If this were our honeymoon I'd find a better place than this run-down motel to make love to you. Right now, I'm going to take you to our room and then go back for the sandwiches."

"Okay." Her stomach grumbled. "Are we still

playing at being a couple?"

"That depends on where we decide this is or isn't going. We can discuss that later. The desk clerk is mainly going to remember we're newlyweds and I carried you in."

"Oh, I see. That draws attention, like the woman in the purple turban."

"Exactly. When you have to hide in plain sight, this is one way to do it."

Clarissa was more than a little disappointed as her excitement deflated and her thoughts grew serious. This isn't a movie or a romance novel, this is reality. Even if he'd been talking about their honeymoon. Her imagination and desires were making her hear what she wanted to hear.

"You got quiet," he said.

"I'm just hungry."

He'd carried her to the far end of the motel and pulled the key out of his back pocket. After opening the door to their room and carrying her inside, he closed the door. "I'm not sure I want to put you down." He placed her on the bed and then leaned over her with one hand on each side of her. "A kiss before I go?"

She nodded and he leaned in and kissed her, soft, short, and sweet, like they might've had on a first date. She thought, *this is our first date, a never-ending one. Most people aren't thrown together before getting to know each other first. Most people aren't kissing each other constantly on a first date.*

"I'm just going to get the sandwiches and drinks. I have a key, so don't open the door for anyone."

"Yes, sir."

"Hey, none of that 'sir' business. I don't need to command you, and you don't need that, either. It's just Warren."

"Okay. Yes, Warren." Sir or not, his commanding way had her wanting to follow him. It was another first for her, she'd learned not to do that with any man, but with him things were changing.

"I'll hurry back." He searched her eyes. "Don't be worrying."

He turned and went out the door, closing it behind him.

She briefly brought her fingers to her lips, savoring the feeling his kiss had left, and then she let her arm fall back down on the bed. The bed was soft and her tired body didn't want to move, so she stayed as he'd placed her and closed her eyes.

Hearing a bag rustling near her ear, she opened her eyes again. "Hello, sleepy. You nodded right off. Once we eat, you can go back to sleep."

"I'm surprised I fell asleep, as hungry as I am."

"Exhaustion can do that." He helped her sit up and then handed her an open water bottle. "Drink up. You're probably dehydrated too."

The water tasted tremendously good. She took another drink and then noticed the Harley parked inside the motel room. "Um, why is the Harley in here?"

"Someone might be tempted to steal it, and it will draw too much attention, especially if they know to look for us on a bike."

"Oh, I see." She took a bite of her sandwich.

"How did you get the bike in here without waking me up?"

Shrugging, he said, "I rolled her in quietly. You were sound asleep."

"Well, I'm glad you woke me. I was starved. I wish I'd eaten more at Pete's."

He nodded. "You were nervous. Now that you're safe here, you can relax. You'll be able to sleep and your appetite will come back." He grinned, "Looks like it already has." She'd devoured half her sandwich while he was talking. "Hungry, I see." His eyes were laughing.

When she finished her sandwich, he asked, "Still hungry?" She nodded. "I can go out again."

She leaned forward. "No. Please, I don't want you to leave again tonight."

"All right, sweetheart. I'm not going anywhere. You can go back to sleep."

Her shoulders relaxed again and she reached for a napkin to wipe her fingers. "I'm going to clean up before I go to sleep."

"Take a shower, if you want. I'll just be here watching TV." He picked up the remote and turned it on.

She got up and went into the bathroom. She turned on the water and took a steamy shower, which made her feel clean, warm, and sleepier than ever. When she got out, she found a toothbrush and toothpaste, which he must've placed by the sink, and brushed her teeth. She'd never even known he'd entered the room. *It might've been nice if he'd taken a shower with me…if I wasn't so tired.* Tired she was, however, and sleep was all she wanted now. Well, maybe it wasn't all she wanted, but it was all she had the energy for.

Wrapped in a towel, she walked back into the room as Warren looked up. "Want another one of my T-shirts to sleep in?" he asked. "I have a clean one in my bag." He handed her a green cotton T-shirt, which was going to be long on her. Then he grinned. "Can I watch?"

They always want to watch. It reminded her too much of how her ex had expected her to perform.

Her face fell just enough for Warren to notice, and he swung his legs over the side of the bed and stood. "I'm only teasing you. Going to get my shower now." He turned to the television screen on the wall and said, "Television on. Set to relaxing beach and waves." The screen changed to a white sandy beach with soft waves rolling in and the quiet sound of the surf. "Television done." He turned to Clarissa. "There you go. Get some rest."

Too tired and confused to figure him out, or herself and what she really wanted, she dropped the towel as soon as he entered the bathroom and pulled his T-shirt on. Climbing into bed, she pulled up the covers. She listened to the water on the television screen and the water running in the shower as she imagined him soaping his body and how she might help him. Those thoughts had her warm by the time he emerged from the bathroom with a towel wrapped around his body.

Her jaw nearly dropped. Those abs and muscular thighs, combined with that small, white towel wrapped around what she could only imagine was as sexy as the rest of him, made her speechless.

He picked up his clothes and went back to the

bathroom. Good thing he hadn't asked her anything, as all words had gone right out of her head. In their place were images of them in bed together. She felt as nervous as a new bride, but they hadn't even determined if they'd be sleeping together. They hadn't determined anything about their relationship, at all. He'd saved her, they'd kissed, and now they were here. It all seemed quite surreal.

Her mantra about men and beaches seemed to have fled too. He emerged again in briefs and a T-shirt and she couldn't help but look. *Oh yes, he's well put together, and it looks like he's not immune to me after all.*

He got under the covers beside her and leaned on his elbow, propped his head on his hand, to look down at her with a smile. "Hello, pretty girl. Feel better, now?"

"Yes." She smiled back at him, shyly. "Are you feeling...sleepy?"

"No, but we both need a good night's sleep, so we can get going early in the morning." He watched her for a moment and then reached out to smooth her hair. She let his gentle hand relax her as he continued stroking her hair for a few minutes. "So soft," he said. "Silky." She smiled, feeling like a cat ready to purr. He smoothed the long, golden strands that had fanned out on her pillow. "Such pretty hair. It's a shame we have to change it."

"Change it?" She frowned, pulled from her drowsy state.

"Yes. I should've told you before you got in the shower, I could've gone and picked up scissors and dye somewhere."

"Scissors?" Her eyebrows rose and she was fully awake now. "Dye?"

"Yes. You need to either cut it or color it. Preferably both."

"You've got to be kidding!" She sat up in bed, her hands flying to cup her hair on both sides of her head. "You're not cutting my hair." She shook her head. "And I'm not coloring it!"

"It's too risky to take you to a salon. We'll have to do it ourselves."

"I'm not changing my hair." Her frown grew fiercer. "Not for anyone."

Cheater Joe had always been after her to "polish her image," as he'd put it; go blonder; get a Brazilian wax, and get a boob job. He'd wanted her in a double D, never mind it would put her whole body out of balance. Hair was the one thing she'd kept changing for him, and she was never going to do it again for a man.

"You need to make it harder for them to find you."

She crossed her arms. "Absolutely not."

"Clarissa, be reasonable."

"I said no." With that, she flipped over, bunched up the pillow, and pulled the sheet over herself.

She balled the sheet in her fist as she lay on her side. *No men, just sand and beach.* And just like that, she had her mantra back.

* * * *

Restless, Warren woke early, as was his habit when he had so much on his mind. He glanced at the clock and then at the beauty by his side. Peaceful in sleep, she appeared younger, and worry-free, unlike the testy and stress-filled woman she'd been last night. Letting her stay in her peaceful slumber, he rose, being careful not to wake her.

Coffee.

He needed coffee. He reached for his jeans and carried them into the bathroom, where he opened up the coffeemaker, surprised by the used condom inside.

Damn it. Damn cheap-ass run-down motels. I sure as hell am not making coffee in that.

He slammed the lid back down, and calmed himself again, hoping the noise didn't wake her. This day needed to start better than yesterday had ended.

Hopefully, she'd be more reasonable about her hair when he brought it up again today. Last night had been bad timing. He should've known she wasn't used to the kind of stress and danger she'd been under, and he should've gone more slowly with her. Apparently, her hair was a touchy subject, and touchy subjects were never good to bring up right before bedtime. Warren could always go back out and get the things they needed, so they could do her hair before they got on the road. It would slow them some, but it was important. He'd bring back breakfast and feed her before bringing the subject up again. Right now, though, he needed to get out of here and find some coffee.

Before he left, he kissed her forehead as she slept and she gave a soft breath and a sigh. Smiling as he watched her, he wished he could wake her slowly, with gentle kisses all over her body. He wondered what other breathy sounds she might make. The urge for coffee interrupted his thoughts again, and he moved to collect his wallet and his gear. It was time to check out the motel grounds, to make sure she was safe, and then he'd go get coffee and breakfast. Warren gave her one last glance, contemplating telling her where he was going.

She's likely exhausted from her ordeal. I'll let her sleep. I'll be back before she even wakes.

He opened the door and eased the Harley out quietly. Outside the room he set the kickstand, and then went back to close the door, making sure it was locked. After walking the motel grounds and seeing nothing out of place, he assured himself she'd be safe until he returned. No one was about this early, and all was quiet. He pushed the bike on down the street away from the motel before he started it, so as not to wake her. God knew a Harley starting up early in the morning would wake everyone nearby. He climbed on and started her up.

Clarissa would sleep until he woke her, and then they'd eat breakfast in the room and talk about her hair. They had to get on down the road after that. It would be best to put as many miles as possible between her and the Atlanta shuttle station. Where they'd be looking for her.

He had to talk her into either cutting or dying her hair, preferably, both. It would be a shame, because her blonde tresses were lovely enough to turn heads.

That's the problem. She's far too memorable. She's the kind of woman a man doesn't easily forget.

Pete had even given her a nickname already. It was on the piece of paper tucked in the bag with the sandwiches. Goldfinch. It suited her. Once any woman was under the protection of the Deep Nest members, she was given a nickname. None of them would be using her real name from this point on. When any of the men in Deep Nest heard a bird or butterfly name, they knew to take special care of that woman. Though just as likely to come to any woman's defense, some women worked for the other side and were likely to turn deadly.

Hero to the rescue thinking had landed more than one of the team members into tight and dangerous spots.

Though Deep Nest would protect and defend any who were standing up against the current status quo, men were not problematic like some of the women had proved to. Pete's theory on that was, men in trouble didn't bring o the rescue the damsel feelings and urges in a man that a woman created by being in trouble. That could be used to manipulate a man. Women who turned on the men of Deep Nest were quickly renamed Canary. Canary Robin had been his downfall and got him shot, though he could only blame himself for that one. Clarissa was different. Guileless. Sweet Clarissa. *Goldfinch.*

Warren grinned. Yes, she was like a bright, pretty bird. With a soft, sweet voice. Soon, he'd be waking her and her voice would be like music to his ears.

He'd need to check in with the team soon and find out if they'd been able to retrieve her stash of seeds before someone from the Benjamin team got there first. Benjamin Innovative Genetics had swift teams once they went into action. Hopefully nothing Clarissa had done or said triggered a response causing them to go in. If they hadn't gone in, she'd move up on the list of fugitives and could even have a bounty on her head. For now though, Warren and Clarissa would maintain silence.

Once he took her to a safe place where they couldn't find her, they could relax. He knew just the place. In the meantime, they needed to be on the move.

After stopping at a gas station, he filled the tank on the bike and picked up a box of doughnuts, two bottles of water, and two large cups of coffee. He was paying at the counter, and had just taken a sip of his coffee.

Boom.

The noise startled Warren and the attendant and they jumped.

Warren spun on his heel and was out the door, looking in the direction of the explosion as flames reached up into the sky.

Clarissa.

He ran to the bike, stuffed the doughnuts and water into the saddlebag, then threw a leg over the Harley and fired it up. The coffee stood abandoned at the counter, as well as in his thoughts. As he raced back to the motel, he prayed she was safe and that they hadn't collected her. If only he could get there in time.

CHAPTER SIX

A loud boom woke Clarissa and she sat up in bed, disoriented, just seconds before the fire alarm came on. It took a moment to register she was in the motel bed where she and Warren had crashed last night. She glanced over to where he'd parked the Harley to find it gone.

He'd left. She leaped out of bed and pulled on her jeans. *Where the hell is he?* She glanced about, looking for a note as she shoved her feet into her shoes, but couldn't find one.

She didn't have time to figure out where or why he'd gone, and with the fire alarms going off, she couldn't think. She had no time to comb her hair or brush her teeth, either, so she grabbed her purse, stuffed her lucky hip scarf into the bag, and hurried to the door.

When she glanced out the door to see if it was safe to go out, she saw people running away and two men moving toward the motel, but no firemen. *Where was the fire?* Those men were moving directly toward her room and one of them saw her. She slammed the door and locked it fast.

Oh my God, they're coming for me.

She ran to look out the window on the other side of the bed. Bright, tall flames shot into the sky from where a propane tank had been.

A siren in the distance told her a fire truck was heading her way. She needed to get out before the fire spread and before those men reached her door. *What if someone had set the fire? What would make a propane tank explode? Had someone shot it? Blown it up?* She realized there'd be news crews with cameras, and she couldn't risk being seen.

Rushing back to the window, she opened the curtains and tugged at the window. It wouldn't open. She turned, looking for something to break it with. She grabbed a ceramic lamp and launched it at the window, just to watch the lamp shatter. The window cracked, but that was all. She yanked a drawer from the dresser and hurled it through the window, squeezing her eyes shut as glass shattered around her.

Smokey, hot air blew through the window, and she squinted. Glass was everywhere. She laid the bedspread across the windowsill before pulling herself outside.

No one behind the motel watched her, but she paused, still having a bad feeling about the fire. *I have to get out of here. Before those men find me.*

Frantic to get as far away from the motel as possible, Clarissa ran until she reached the edge of town. She stopped beneath the trees by the side of the road and leaned against a tree trunk to catch her breath. When her heart stopped racing, she checked her coin purse.

Two dollars, not even enough to buy a cup of soup. She had no cash and couldn't use her credit cards without being traced.

She watched and listened to hear if anyone was following her, wondering where the heck Warren was. Where could she go?

A truck with the helping hands of Benjamin Innovative Genetics came down the road. That was it. She could try to hitch a ride, if she could find a truck driven by a human. Most of the trucks drove themselves and it was only old truckers on the roads now, those who owned their own rigs. Soon, they'd be gone too, as all the truck driving schools had closed when auto-drive trucks began to roll out onto the roads in large numbers. She wished the helping hands of Benjamin Innovative Genetics would help her out with a ride, but the truck rolled on past without even slowing down.

A red truck came next, with Vale Trucking on the side and she waved her arms, praying the truck would stop. When there was an actual man in the truck and it pulled over, she went to the driver's window and said, "I need a ride to Jacksonville. Can you help me?"

"You've got it." The grey-haired cowboy smiled. "Climb on in, little lady."

She smiled back. "Thank you."

"Name's Cody Vale, and you're quite welcome, darlin'."

She climbed into the passenger's side and noted the truck smelled like peaches. Pulling her seatbelt across her body and hooking it, she said, "I really do appreciate this. My ride left me and I need to go see my sister. I'm Clar – I mean sister Sue." She caught herself before giving her real name away.

"But not a nun I take it."

She shook her head. "No."

"Well, sister Sue. Glad I was headed that way." He reached behind her and she tensed, unsure what he was reaching for or what he'd do. His hand came back holding a peach. "Peach?"

"Oh!" Surprised, she laughed. "Why, yes, thank you." Nobody she knew had fresh peaches, they were expensive and hard to come by.

He handed it to her with a grin. "Thought I might be goin' for somethin' else, didn't ya?"

"I wasn't too sure."

"A lady alone in her travels cain't be too careful."

She held the peach, hungry, but nervous. *He's right. What was I thinking, hitching a ride with a complete stranger? What if he'd had a gun back there and pulled it on me?* "You're right." She gave a nervous laugh.

He reached for another peach and brought it forward. "These here peaches are mighty good. They're from my brother-in-law's farm, he keeps me stocked."

"If they're as good as they smell, they must be delicious." She took a bite and the sweet juice made her close her eyes for a moment.

"Yep," Mr. Vale said. "Mighty good."

She thought of Warren again and wondered where the heck he was. *Why did he run out on me? How could he do that to me?* She didn't understand, and it hurt. She'd fallen for him and fallen fast and he'd made a fool out of her. Just ran off and left her. Just like that. It stung. But it wouldn't happen again.

She pushed him out of her mind. She was on her own now. It was best not to dwell on it. She remembered her mantra and repeated it to herself. *No men, just sand and beach.*

She glanced at the truck driver who was enjoying

his peach as he drove.

They ate in silence as they headed down the road, and it reminded her of being with one of her aunt's friends. After living in the city, she'd forgotten what being with country folks felt like. There were few things as sweet in life as the taste of a juicy peach and the silence of a comfortable friend. It made her want to close her eyes again to savor the moment.

When Mr. Vale stopped for gas, she went looking for the ladies' room.

A bald man with a strong chin and nose came up to her, his grey eyes concerned. "I wonder, miss, if you could help me out? My wife isn't feeling well. She went into the ladies' room. Can you help me? Could you check on her?"

"Sure. What's her name?"

"Brenda." The man moved closer to the ladies' room door. "I really appreciate this."

"No problem." She opened the door and went inside calling, "Brenda?"

Though the stalls looked empty, she pushed the door open on each one. No Brenda. His wife either hadn't made it to the ladies' room or she'd left.

Clarissa hurried to do her business and then washed and was just coming out the door to tell the man his wife wasn't inside.

He stood just in the doorway of a back door to the building, which led outside. Had he figured out his wife wasn't in the ladies' room and was out there looking for her? She hurried over to tell him.

"Oh, mister?" she called to him.

Just as she did he stepped out and closed the door, not hearing her.

She pushed the door open and looked for him. Seeing him, she stepped out and said, "I looked for her but there's no one else in the ladies…"

Before she could finish, a hand holding a cloth came over her mouth cutting off her air along with the ability to yell and then the prick of a needle went into her arm. Her world suddenly went sideways.

Everything went dark.

Groggy, she woke, turning her head from side to side, moaning, but unable to make a noise with the cloth gag in her mouth preventing it.

Oh my God, where am I? Her thoughts began to race and her heart along with them.

A scream of panic worked its way up her throat but had nowhere to go and something rough, some kind of blanket or cloth was covering her head and body so she couldn't see. Nauseous, and more than a bit thirsty, likely from the shot he'd given her, the gag stuck to her dry tongue and she wanted a drink of water more than she ever had in her life. Dear God, but she was thirsty.

How long have I been like this? Where am I, and where are they taking me?

She was in a vehicle of some kind, could feel the road and the occasional bump along with a radio playing hard rock. Then it stopped and her stomach stopped roiling. She closed her eyes and pretended to be asleep as she listened, in case someone was coming to check on her.

A door opened and she felt the air change as a gust of cool wind blew inside. *Air.* She wanted air. *And water.* Hands wrapped around her bound ankles and dragged her out of the vehicle. Maybe it was a truck. It had a bench type seat and a door. Either the truck or the back seat of a car. She couldn't tell.

Then he was hoisting her over his shoulder and her head hung down, blood rushing to it and she thought she might throw up into the gag as her stomach roiled again. The rough blanket fell away from her face and she breathed in air at last.

"She ain't covered," a man's voice said.

"Don't matter," another replied, "now she's here she ain't going nowhere."

Neither voice was familiar.

"Put her in the guest bedroom," the man who'd asked her to check on his wife directed the men, "she's awake."

It was a trap, she thought. *I fell for it. I was so stupid.*

The man carrying her turned and she saw the man who'd tricked her.

"Hello, darlin'." He grinned. "Now be a good girl. I'm going to remove the gag," he said. "No one can hear you, now, even if you do scream."

She was close to panic as she woke a bit more and her thoughts raced. *Warren. I need Warren. If only he would come and rescue…*

The words died as she remembered. *Warren wasn't coming.* Warren had ridden off and left her. *He wasn't coming back.*

What did these men want? How could she get out of this? *I have to get away from these men.*

Once the gag was out, she gave a dry rasp, "I'm not going to scream. Please, I need water."

"And water you shall have. Once we have you settled."

She was plunked onto a double bed and rolled over onto her belly. A man with a scar across his left cheek like he'd been burned untied her legs and she held still, hoping he'd untie her hands next. Not knowing his name, she nicknamed him Scar.

Maybe if she went along with Scar for now, he'd let her go. Maybe they wouldn't harm her. *What did they want?*

His hands spread her legs and then he tied one leg to the bedpost.

Oh no. Her hope sunk. He wasn't untying her.

He flipped her over again and reached for her other leg. She watched him taking in every detail. Short brown hair and blue eyes. Big, beefy hands and a scar that crossed his jaw. Yes, she could pick him out of a line-up. But wait. That wasn't good. He didn't care if she saw his face. He didn't care at all. His face held no expression.

Then the other man came toward her with a needle.

No, no, no. She began to thrash. But they held her down and the needle went in.

Dizziness again and that sick feeling.

They untied her hands, propped a few pillows

beneath her head and then one of them put a glass of water to her lips. She drank, slowly, her senses groggy again.

The next time she woke she was naked. Naked and tied to the bed in a spread eagle. She looked slowly around the room as her senses became clearer. The bed was damp in places. A can of shaving cream and a razor sat on the bed stand along with a towel. Her skin chilled and goose bumps spread along with the realization they'd shaved her. Legs, underarms and down below. What had they done to her and why were they doing this?

The bald man entered the room and said, "Good you're awake. You got to eat something."

"What do you want? Why am I here?"

"You're going to be a wealthy wife soon. Once you're prepared."

"Whose wife? You or one of your goons?"

"Whose wife?" The man laughed. "Why the one who values you the most. You're quite valuable. More than you know. Green eyes are rare. How much do you think you'll bring?"

"I'm worth $150 a minute, $3,000 minimum for weddings."

He laughed. "You amuse me. Let's hope you amuse your future husband as much. One hundred fifty a minute, what an imagination."

"You're planning to sell me to a hopeful groom?" She laughed though much of her laughter was nervous. The laughter shook her belly. She noted he watched it rippling with interest. "You have no idea who you just captured—and no idea of my value."

"Oh, yes," he laughed again, "I know your value. These men pay high prices for green-eyed blondes with curves like yours."

"Of course, they do," she agreed. "I've been making them pay me for years."

"You're a whore."

She laughed again. "No, I don't sleep with men. I make them pay me, but I never even have to take my clothes off."

He crossed his arms and frowned at her again. "Crazy talk. No man pays a woman for that."

"They do if she's a belly dancer," she sang the words. "You'd be surprised at the things I can do."

"Huh." The light had come into his eyes now, though, as he was catching on. "You make this much just dancing."

"Yes, I do. I'm a professional belly dancer."

"I don't believe you."

"I'll show you, if you'll untie me?"

"Maybe." He left the room. He'd been silent, but his body language and expression had told her he was considering it.

When he came back, he tossed the red and gold hip scarf on the bed, the coins jangled as it landed. He pointed to it. "This is what you do? You dance with this?"

She nodded. "It has great value to me." All the

sincerity she had went into that statement. "This is what I dance with. I'll need some kind of clothes, I don't dance in the nude."

He nodded and she knew he was intrigued. She'd have to keep him convinced of her high value. It was the only way to survive. Her lucky red hip scarf might save her life if she could just pull this off until she could get away from the crazy bald guy.

"You will dance for me now and then we'll see."

"I don't dance nude."

"You will this time. Only wearing that." He pointed to the hip scarf.

"Untie me and I'll dance."

He untied her and she pulled her arms and legs in to cover herself. She reached for her hip scarf and then tied it around her waist. Sitting up she felt a wave of dizziness. How she'd stand and dance she didn't know, but she knew she'd be dancing for her life.

He'd put on some music for her and she'd just managed to distract the bald man with her dancing when a curse came from the other room and then a man shouted, "Stop."

"Felicia, run!" she heard a woman scream.

The bald man turned and went out the door fast, slamming it behind him. Relieved he'd gone away she reached for a bed sheet and wrapped it around herself wondering what to do next and where she could go if she slipped out that door. She went to the window and looked out. A woman was running into the woods.

Then she heard a shot and the woman fell.

She sunk onto the bed. All hope of escaping gone.

****

Clarissa stared out from behind the curtains, past the stage to the men seated at tables near the edge. Dark swarthy men with beards, and wearing Arabic clothing, some of the men in suits. Men who were important to Mr. Peason from the way he greeted them.

These guys were used to strippers. Belly dancers like her were treated with more respect than strippers, though they didn't make as much money. Clarissa drew a fine line between dancing and sleeping with the men she danced for, as most belly dancers did. They only time she'd broken that rule, she'd ended up married to Joe and that hadn't worked out so well.

Clarissa loved to dance and had since she was a young girl. She'd have danced if no one were there to see her. But she couldn't dance the way she wanted to now. She had a role to play. She had to dance in a way that satisfied men who were used to strippers and please them without taking her clothes off. This could be quite a challenge if any of the men became insistent upon wanting more. She'd never performed without an escort or a guard nearby and wasn't sure where Mr. Peason would stand if one of his clients wanted her badly enough. She touched her lucky hip scarf and prayed luck would be with her tonight.

* * * *

Warren couldn't find Clarissa anywhere. Hazlehurst was a small town, and he'd run out of people to ask and places to look. If no one had seen her, she must've either skipped town, or they'd found her and taken her away. That wasn't something he wanted to think about. *If she'd left town, how had she done it?* There was no train or bus that had come through today, and he doubted she had enough money for a ticket, even if there had been.

Out of ideas and filled with frustration, he called Pete and quickly informed him of what had happened. He didn't mention her real name as they spoke in codes and word associations.

"Goldfinch has flown out of sight," Pete said. "But we'll find her."

"Damn it," Warren's voice rose along with his frustration. "There are too many cats out there hunting for birds. We need to find her now."

"We'll find her."

"We'd better."

"I want her found as much as you do, mate," Pete said.

That's doubtful, Warren thought. *This is more than a job or a mission, this is now personal.* That sweet little birdy had captured a piece of his heart in less than forty-eight hours. Not knowing where she was or if she was safe was driving him crazy.

When Warren didn't respond, Pete spoke again, "I'll let you know the minute I hear something. Catch you later."

Warren hung up and turned to look at highway seventy-five. It was a road he'd soon be back on, this time alone. He missed Clarissa's soft hands clutching him and moving in closer when she got nervous.

He missed her, he'd already grown attached. He couldn't deal with that right now, though. He needed to focus.

Find her, retrieve her, and keep her safe. With the

Deep Nest network keeping eyes and ears open for Clarissa, hopefully he'd find her fast, before anything bad happened. *Why did she run instead of waiting for me? She must be scared out there, scared and alone, with no money or way to protect herself.*

The thought tore at him and he wished she had a gun to protect herself with. He'd bet, however, that she didn't know how to shoot. She'd seemed afraid of the gun when she'd seen it.

Warren climbed onto the Harley and fired it up before roaring down the road. Somehow, he was going to find her, and he wouldn't stop until he did.

CHAPTER SEVEN

Clarissa now despaired of ever getting away from Mr. Peason, the man who'd taken her. He kept her under lock and key when she wasn't dancing, and she'd now seen several girls come and go from his home, where they were kept sedated more often than not until they were sold. Time ran together and Clarissa wasn't sure how long she'd been there. Some days she'd tried to block from her memory entirely.

Felicia, the one girl who'd fought back and nearly escaped had been shot. From that point on the men talked about their "doll" which replaced the inflatable doll jokes. The other girls had been forced to watch as two of the men "played" with the woman, while she slowly died of her bullet wounds. Then one day Felicia's body was just gone from the house and no one ever spoke of her again.

The only plus for Clarissa, other than the fact she was still alive, was the fact she was dancing, and dancing at the Lounging Lizard was the only time she now felt truly alive. She watched as Mr. Peason greedily counted the money from tonight's show and his profile reminded her of a toad, the way he'd hunched down in his seat. It was positively reptilian.

Turning his greedy eyes to hers, he said, "Two shows next weekend. I'm adding a midnight special. Have some important clients coming to town."

She nodded and said, "Good take tonight. I'm hungry. I'd like a steak, baked potato, a salad and dessert."

The greedy miser, who only fed the women chicken rice soup with crackers, every night of the week, narrowed his eyes at her. Steak was more like what he ate. The women were nothing but livestock to him, and he'd only feed them something cheap and easy, to keep them alive before he sold them. "Why?"

"You want me to keep my strength up, don't you? Instead of collapsing on stage? I'm an athlete. I need protein and carbs." She didn't doubt he viewed her as only slightly more valuable than the women he sold. But, she'd get out of him what she could. It was all about survival now, and she was hungry for real food. Dancing made her hungry.

He grunted. "We'll see."

Confident he'd actually feed her something decent, she smiled at him. "Thank you." He couldn't know that in her head she'd added, you nasty toad.

There were eleven girls in the house now, not counting Clarissa. Where he got them all, she didn't know. It must be easier for girls to disappear than anyone knew, because he never got caught, and he never seemed scared. She wondered how much money he made, and what he did with it. The house had heavy dark out curtains that never opened, and inside, bars on the windows. Each of the four bedrooms had two twin beds with iron shackles, and he'd added two more in what would have been a dining room, and now two more in the living room behind the couch, where she slept. He now had twelve girls counting Clarissa. She was the only one allowed out of the shackles and they were placed back on when they returned from the club.

She had those few hours of freedom. The time to dress for the club and do her hair and makeup, the ride to the club, the performance time, the ride home from the club, time for a quick shower and she too had to be chained to her bed.

Whatever Mr. Peason was planning had something to do with midnight and twelve girls. So, the number twelve must be important. He wanted her dancing a second show at midnight. She wished she knew more about what he'd planned and how it involved her. It would involve her because she was the twelfth girl. In a perfect world, she'd get herself and all these girls out of here. But this wasn't a perfect world. She couldn't even figure out how to get herself out of here. So how could she help anyone else?

This situation called for someone with Warren's kind of skills. Mr. Peason had men watching the house and the club. There wasn't one moment when someone wasn't watching. For maybe the hundredth time since he'd taken her and locked her in this inescapable hell, she wished Warren or someone like him would come and get her out.

Oh, who was she kidding? She wanted Warren.

Warren, where are you? And why did you leave me?

* * * *

Pete and Warren were both at the Dark Nest local meeting place leaning over an unfolded map on the table. A rarity, because printed maps were hard to find, this one, showed old abandoned roads that didn't show up on the computerized GPS system. Warren ran a hand through his hair in frustration and said, "How can she have just disappeared? She has very little street smarts to pull that off, completely vanishing with no one seeing her. As healthy and bright eyed as she is, she ought to stand out."

Pete shook his head. "I don't know, mate. Maybe she has more skills than you realize. Or maybe she had a friend help her. That's more likely because I think you're right. She doesn't seem like the type to be able to navigate out on the street with no money and no transportation. She's got nothing to trade, except herself."

Warren banged his fist on the table. "Damn it." He stood and paced. The last thing he wanted to think of was Clarissa trading her body on the streets. "Damn it all to hell."

Sam entered the room and they both looked at him. "I think I found her," he said. "She's dancing at a bar just a few hour's drive from where you left her."

"I didn't fucking leave her."

"To get coffee you did."

Sam was the most direct man on their team and he'd call you on your shit every time. Warren couldn't argue that point with him. "I was coming back."

"I know ya were, mate, but she didn't," Pete said.

"Where is she?" Warren growled, wanting to hit something or someone.

"Place is called the Lounging Lizard."

"Great. Just great." Warren shook his head. *What kind of fucking name is that? Lizards. More like the men are wolves and she is the lamb they are after.* "Son of a bitch. What the hell is she doing back on a stage? I told her not to stand out."

"You'd better hurry," Sam said. "If we've found

her, they can too, and they may not be far behind."

Warren grabbed his leather jacket off the back of the seat and headed for the door.

"You want to take some back up?" Pete called after him.

"No." And he went out the door.

Outside the weather was brisk and he pulled on the jacket and strode to the motorcycle. Throwing a leg over, he pulled the key out of his pocket and went to fire it up.

What the hell was she thinking?

With a roar, the bike was out onto the street and headed for the highway.

****

The Lounging Lizard was a stand-alone bar. A giant, green lizard with glowing, red eyes sat atop the roof. Warren had the urge to shoot it, which was ridiculous, this was no living Godzilla for people to fear.

The stress of Clarissa having been missing for three weeks, lay at the core of his anger. He needed to focus, she was in the bar and he needed to get her out and to a safe place.

He stepped inside and glanced about. She was in the bar, all right; half-dressed, shimmying and dancing on a small stage. With her long, blonde hair, that red hip scarf with three rows of gold coins jingling and catching the light as she shook her hips, and a sheer red skirt with slits all the way up each side showing her legs. He couldn't miss her. *Damn, that woman can really move her hips, and those legs, wow.* Mad as he was, the sight of just how skilled she was with her body made him pause.

Every man in the place was likely thinking of either watching her move those hips as she rode him or pinning those hips down to stop them from moving as he took her. Extricating her from the bar wouldn't be easy. She was the main attraction and these men had paid to see her.

"That's a fifty-dollar cover," said the beefy man on a stool in the narrow entryway.

Not a good exit route, Warren thought as he pulled out three twenties and handed them over. His gaze took in the exit sign in the back of the room as he evaluated how he'd get Clarissa out of there in a worst-case scenario.

She hadn't noticed him yet, her attention was on the men closest to the stage with bills in their hands. A man stood, shouted something in Arabic, and threw dollar bills over her head. Six other Arabic men sat at the table, wearing red and white head coverings and white robes. She smiled at the men and kept dancing.

Moving closer, Warren could see her skirt was see-through. The men could see her long legs clear up to her red panties, and her bra-like top wasn't covering much, either. One of the Arabic men leered and grabbed his crotch. Clarissa's face blanched a little, but she kept dancing as if they weren't being offensive, as if she did this all the time and it was nothing new.

He wanted to yank her off that stage and rip their heads off. *What these animals will do to her, she has no idea. She is like a lamb to be slaughtered and she doesn't even seem to know it. These are the wolves that will tear her apart. But she has a sheep dog here now.* He had to get her out of here. This might be the good old United States of America, but slavery still existed here, and Arabs were notorious for buying women. Deep Nest had turned up what looked like the kind of club where such women were auctioned.

Warren moved through the room, trying to force his anger back, it took everything he had.

Clarissa's number had ended and a bald man holding a cigar, with a puffed-up attitude announced she'd return after a short break. He was answered by boos, but he held up his hand and the crowd quieted. He told them drinks were available and her grand finale would be worth waiting for. Then there would be a special midnight show.

Warren didn't want to think what that might consist of, but from the man's tone he could imagine. He had to find her now and make sure she didn't step back on that stage. *What the hell is she thinking, dancing in a place like this?* If word got back to the government she was here, they'd have her out of there and in a much worse place—if they didn't kill her first, which was most likely.

Down the gloomy hallway, which stank of cigar smoke, he spotted the bald guy talking to one of his henchmen. Warren kept out of sight and listened.

"I want you to go out there and spread the word. Tell all those Arabs out there she's top dollar. If they don't plan to bid big money tonight then don't bid. Nowhere else they're gonna find a green eyed, blonde, belly dancer. She's a high value woman and I won't settle for less."

The henchman nodded and Warren moved away as he headed down the hall toward him. But not before he'd noted what must be the dressing room where Clarissa likely was, and where the bald guy had gone.

Once the henchman had moved into the main

room, Warren went back down the hall and listened outside the dressing room door to them arguing.

"I'm not changing clothes while you're in here, so unless you want me to be late on stage, I suggest you step out," Clarissa said.

"Listen you dumb blonde, you don't seem to understand. I *own* you, and I'm the one you need to please. If you don't want a good beating, you'd better get your ass out there."

"No, you don't understand. They want a show, and I'm the only one you have who can give it to them. Did you hear those men? They want me out there dancing and they aren't patient. If I go out and tell them I can't perform because you won't let me change, you'll answer to them."

Listening, Warren grinned. *Well, my girl has spunk, after all. Good for you, Clarissa.*

The man spoke again. "You'll be answering to one of them soon enough. In the meantime, you'll do as I say. I can send you out buck naked right now if I decide to. I own you."

"Why did you tell them there's a special midnight show? There won't be any midnight show unless you're going to start paying me."

The sound of a loud smack carried through to where Warren waited, listening. Hearing it, he was angry enough to kill the man who'd captured his Goldfinch.

He stepped away from the door and sure enough, seconds later, the bald guy came barreling out, pissed, and slammed the door behind him. Seeing Warren he growled, "Who the fuck are you?"

Warren punched him in the throat hitting his larynx.

The bald man gasped for breath and staggered back.

Warren wrapped both arms around the man's neck and chin, locking them, and with a sharp twist snapped his neck.

No one had heard or seen them. Warren quickly picked the body up, opened the door, carried the man inside, and dumped him on a lumpy couch, much to Clarissa's surprise.

She stood with her mouth in an "O" and her bra open in the back as she clasped it to her breasts, frozen in shock at seeing him.

"Good to see you," he said, "although I'd like to see a little less of you right now. Do you have any other clothes? Anything less revealing?"

She burst into tears and he moved toward her, taking hold of her arms, holding her steady to calm her. "You're okay," he said. "I'm taking you out of here. Now. We need to get you covered. Dressed."

She stood staring at him. Then she reached out to touch his chest, pressing on it, checking to see if he was real. "You're here," she whispered, tears rolling down her face, staring at him as if she couldn't believe he was real.

"I'm here." He nodded. "Let's go." They didn't have time for this right now. He gave her his most commanding tone and look. "Now."

She seemed to shake herself and then listen to him as she started to move toward a rack where flimsy garments hung.

As she slipped her arms into a long, black, silk robe, he said, "You're wearing that?"

"It's all I have," she said. "Mr. Peason wouldn't let me have anything else."

"Wouldn't let you," he frowned. "Where the hell are your clothes, your jeans and jacket and the T-shirt I gave you?"

In a very small voice, she said, "He took them."

"Come on." He grabbed her hand. "We're getting the hell out of here."

Out the door and down the hallway, they were heading through the exit just as someone in the bar saw her leaving and shouted, "Hey, Goldie Touch! Where are ya going?"

It was a good thing he'd parked the Harley out back, because he had her on it and fired the bike up just as the bald man's henchmen men started to pour out of the bar.

He could feel her shivering against the night wind, as the silk robe did little to cover her. Angry, he raced faster, but then he started to slow down. This wasn't fair to her, she was back there, freezing, while he was working his anger out.

He pulled over and they got off the bike. "Here," he said, and pulled off his black T-shirt. "You're freezing."

"The wind is kinda cold back there," she said, her teeth chattering.

He helped her with the robe and then slipped the

T-shirt over her head. "Think you can lose that coin belt now?" She shook her head.

He watched and wanted to throttle her. *God, what am I going to do with this woman? She is so exasperating.* She stood there, shivering in his T-shirt looking helpless and adorable. How could he stay mad at her when she was looking at him like that? And she was cold.

"We'll just put it in the saddlebag and keep it safe." He shook his head sadly, "Once again, you've drawn attention and made yourself memorable. Dancing in a club. What the hell were you thinking? It's only a matter of time before they find you, unless we change some things."

"What about my skirt?"

He eyed it and proceeded to take a knife from his pocket. Lifting the skirt up, he cut the material until the skirt ended just below her butt. Giving her a pat on her left butt cheek, which made her jump and giggle, he said, "They can see everything, anyway, but now there's less red flying in the wind to catch their eyes."

She giggled again and rubbed the cheek he'd patted, her eyes bright. "Your hand is warm."

Watching her reaction, which was out of place given the circumstances, he said, "You must like a good spanking." Her face turned red, but she didn't deny it. "Or it's nerves making you giggle. You're not making it easy for me to do my job, you know."

She frowned. "Your job? I'm not your job…and, anyway, you left me." Her voice rose and she looked like she was about to start crying again. "You left me."

"I went to get us breakfast."

"Guess you had to lay the damn eggs." He could see her anger below the surface, anger and hurt. Now the nervous giggles were gone, replaced with her true feelings.

"I wasn't gone that long. I got gas and doughnuts and I was on my way back." Exasperation filled him. "I'd never just up and leave you. What kind of man do you think I am?"

Realization spread across her face. "I didn't know." She stood there, blinking away the tears that had gathered but not fallen, and looked both clueless and irresistible.

"You didn't know? I've have done nothing but see to your safety since I met you, and you thought I'd just leave you at a motel in the middle of nowhere?" The more he spoke, the angrier he got.

"There was no note," she spoke in a soft voice that nearly broke. "And you were gone." She turned away and frowned as she spoke, her words coming, "I had to break a window to get out of the motel, and that fire, I think the people who are after me set it." She caught her breath and then let it out again. "And there were men headed toward my room and you weren't there and I didn't know what to do." Her voice grew louder. "You weren't there."

Hearing that pushed away any thoughts of wanting to shake some sense into her. Now, he only wanted to pull her near. She'd been afraid and alone, and she thought she still was.

"Well, I am here now," he spoke firmly. Taking her by the shoulders and pulling her close, he looked into her eyes and said, "I would never leave you. I had no way of leaving you a note, you were sound asleep and I didn't want to wake you. I was coming right back and I thought you'd be safe. That was my mistake, I won't make it again."

"I'm glad you're here now," she said, blinking back tears. "It's been hard trying to make it on my own. First there was the fire, and then Mr. Peason kidnapped me. It's been so hard."

"I know," he said. "You were brave, though, and you did it all yourself. You're stronger than you know."

Her shoulders started to shake, even with him holding her, and her lip trembled before the words came tumbling out. "Mr. Peason kept me and the other girls locked in a house. He shackled us to our beds. One of the girls tried to escape the second day I was there and they shot her and then did bad things to her while she died. After that the other girls were never left unshackled. The only time I was allowed out was to dance. The other girls were never allowed out. He kept giving them shots of something." She shivered and searched his eyes. "Dance was the only bargaining chip I had." He held her and listened, watching as a tear rolled down her cheek and then another, her tears coming out now that her words were coming out. "I think he was going to try to sell me to one of those men from the bar tonight at the special midnight show. Because he wouldn't talk about the new costume anymore, and said I wouldn't need it. I think if you hadn't come tonight I would've been gone. Warren, I was so scared."

She'd been holding her fear in so no one could see it, and now all her emotions were emptying from where she'd stuffed them. He wanted to bring her away from the things she'd been through, so he kissed her. One minute, she was crying, the next, his lips were upon hers, moving slow and gentle.

She caught her breath as she adjusted to the

surprise kiss, but then she responded with passion as well as urgency. The kiss intensified until they both had to come up for air, and she opened her eyes, which now shined at him with desire.

"No one's gonna hurt you, baby." He tucked her hair behind her ear and let his fingers trail down the side of her jaw. "You're with me and you'll be all right. I won't let anyone hurt you."

"I know," her small voice came again.

He smiled and gave her another squeeze. "Are you okay to ride now? I want to get us off the road and to a safe place for the night."

"Yes, I'm okay now and I want that too." She glanced over her shoulder. "But those other women..."

"I'll be calling Pete and will get word back to the brotherhood. We'll get the women out and shut down the club. If you can remember the location of the house, that will help. The special sale at midnight. Was he planning to sell any of the others tonight?

"No. Just me I think because he didn't bring any of the other girls to the club this time."

"Good."

"I don't know where the house is. I was always blindfolded before they moved me back and forth and they tied my wrists."

"I'll call it in as soon as we're far enough away for you to be safe. We've got two hours before the auction is supposed to start, if there's anyone to step into his place to hold it. Even if they tried to auction one of the other girls they'd have to go to the house to get them first and there's a body to deal with now. His death should disrupt their organization and slow things down a bit. We should be able to find the house and get those girls out before there's another auction."

"Oh, I'm glad. I want to get them all out."

"We'll shut down the whole operation. Try not to worry."

"I'll just feel better when I know they're all safe." She started to cry again. "It was horrible. You have no idea."

He gathered her close and hugged her tight. "You're safe and with me now. But we have to get on down the road to keep you safe."

She nodded against his chest. "Okay."

He kissed the top of her head and then pulled away. "Time to go."

She climbed back onto the bike behind him and soon they were roaring down the road together again.

* * * *

They rode an hour and then Warren stopped to refuel the bike at a gas station where two red eighteen-wheelers with the helping hands of the Benjamin Innovative Genetics Corporation were parked. The tagline beneath the hands read, "Helping to make a healthier world." Warren made a call to Pete and turned over the information. He hung up and turned to her. "Team is en route to the club and they will find the house."

"Oh good. I hope the women will be okay."

A truck driver was heading toward his cab when he spotted Warren, interrupting them. "Hey, bud, it's too cold to be out here without a shirt." He climbed into the cab and came back with a T-shirt in his hands. "Here, this ought to fit ya."

"Thanks," Warren said as he took the shirt.

"How about you, lady? Do you want a shirt too?" Clarissa wondered if she'd imagined the strange look that had crossed Warren's face when he unfolded the red T-shirt and saw the image of two open hands, after all, the logo was everywhere, so it was nothing new to see it. "Sure, thank you."

When the man went to his truck, Warren spoke low. "Try not to say too much to him, but stay friendly."

The driver came back and held out a shirt for her. "I thought you'd like pink." She thanked him and he gave them a wave before hurrying back to his truck.

"Come on," Warren said. He'd already put the shirt on and was waiting for her.

"I thought you wanted to get something to eat and drink?"

"Not right now."

She wasn't going to argue with him when she was getting the sense he wanted to get away. It was making her nervous, so she climbed on behind him.

"Those damn hands are everywhere," he said as he started the bike.

About another hour down the road, they stopped at a drug store. Warren didn't say much, but he went straight to the T-shirt section and picked out a tie-dyed shirt. The store also had sundresses, and she eyed them while he was looking at the shirts.

"Go ahead," he said. "Pick the one you like." She picked a blue one with green palm trees that went nearly to her knees. "Perfect," he said. "After we pay, go to the ladies' room and change. Toss the skirt and the pink T-shirt."

"But I haven't even worn it," she protested.

He gave her a stern look and she nodded without arguing further.

They chose snacks, and he paid for the items and went to wait outside by the bike while she went to change.

In the ladies' room, she tossed the red bra and skirt into the trash, glad to be rid of them and anything that would remind her of Mr. Peason, along with the new pink T-shirt. She washed her face, removing all her makeup and freshening up. When she looked in the mirror, she smiled. Just a girl heading to the beach, that's what she looked like now. The red shoes didn't really go with her sundress, but she hadn't thought to ask for flip-flops.

Walking outside, she heard a low whistle. Turning to him, she smiled.

"Very nice," he said. "I think you look better without all that stuff on your face."

"Really?" She tilted her head, giving him a pondering look. Most of the men she'd known liked the made-up, blonde showgirl look on her, but Warren seemed to be just the opposite.

"You look good that way, more natural."

She smiled. "Well, thank you."

"You're welcome." His expression changed again.

"Warren," she asked. "What's wrong?" He hesitated, as if weighing whether to tell her what he was thinking, as if she couldn't handle it. "Please tell me."

"Why blow up the motel?" he said. "It would've been easier to come into the room and take you while I was gone."

"Maybe they didn't know which room I was in, or they didn't know you were gone."

"Sweetheart, if one of them wanted to take you out of that hotel room, they would have. No." he shook his head, "they wanted something more than simply to pick you up for questioning."

"So, you think they wanted something else?"

"Maybe they wanted to make you run, to see what you'd do and where you'd go."

"Maybe I'm not the one they were after, maybe they're after you, because nobody but you has showed up looking for me."

"If they were after me, they'd have sent a large team. They'd know about my training and wouldn't waste men on a failed attempt." He frowned deeper. "I don't like it. They blew up the motel and then went silent, that just doesn't happen unless there's a reason, and now, out of the blue, this trucker gives us T-shirts, like they hand them out every day."

"You make it sound like everything has a reason."

"It does."

"I think the man was just being nice."

115

He held up the T-shirt he'd been given, ripped open the seams, and tore it apart, looking for something.

"I don't understand," she said.

"They could have a bug. You can't trust anything from that company." He shook his head as he pulled apart the bottom seam of the shirt hem and found a small piece of plastic inside. "Who do you think designed Sendot?"

CHAPTER EIGHT

"Wait a minute." She frowned. "The Benjamin Innovative Genetics Corporation designed Sendot? The helping hands people? But they help people."

"No, they don't. That's just their marketing. They help themselves to profit, that's what they do. They create problems with one hand and with the other they sell you something that fixes it."

"Oh, those big hands are everywhere. That's really creepy. Big evil hands."

"So, you can see why I don't trust these T-shirts. There could be listening devices or tracking devices or drugs to knock you out. Anything. They have all the capabilities with the best scientists and God only knows what they're working on now. You said it. BIGC is evil. I agree." He tossed the plastic thing and the shirt in the trash. "And whatever was in that shirt, neither of us are wearing it."

She shivered as goose bumps moved up her body. "So now what do we do?" She wrapped her arms around herself, suddenly chilled.

"Cold?" He put his arm around her and rubbed her arm to warm her. "Well find a place which isn't a motel with a register to sign into. We're going camping."

"Oh. I've never been camping."

"City girl," he teased.

"That's me." She smiled at him. "You'll have to teach me."

"My pleasure." He smiled back.

It felt good to be with him again and she wished they were going on a date, a camping date, instead of being chased by some big evil corporation. The image of those hands was now stuck in her head and they seemed larger and ominous. Though the size of the hands on the sides of the massive trucks they passed hadn't changed, the way she viewed them had.

Two more hours down the road, they stopped at a camping supply store.

"What do we need?" Clarissa asked.

"A tent and a few other things," he said. "Shoes for you, for one."

She sighed, "I hope you're keeping a list of everything I owe you."

"It's taken care of," he said. "Our men were able to retrieve enough seeds from your house to make you a nice nest egg to start over with. Those seeds are valuable."

"If there were no seeds there for the government to find, maybe I'm not on that list, after all. Maybe they'll forget about me."

"They didn't have time to move the plants. Enough of them were found, so yes, you're on the list. I wish you weren't, but you are, and we've verified that. You can't go home again, not while President Garrett is in power...and your ex is missing."

"Missing?" Her voice squeaked. "Do you think they killed him?"

"I have no clue, but they took him and he hasn't been returned."

"Joe knew about my herbs and my aunt, but he doesn't know much about them. He never wanted to know, always told me to shut up when I started talking about it."

"I'm taking you to a place where everyone talks about it." He watched her, gauging her reaction. "No one there will ever tell you to shut up. I think you'll like it."

"Where?"

"I can't tell you, in case you're captured, but I can tell you you'll be able to grow herbs. Now that we have your seeds, you can continue your family's tradition."

"That's wonderful." She smiled. "I'm so glad the seeds were saved."

After getting everything they needed, they went to the check out.

"I've never been camping before," she said.

"You're going to love it," the clerk said. "Where are you going?" Clarissa froze. *Oh, no. I opened my big mouth.*

"It's a surprise," Warren said with a wink. "Our one-year anniversary is next month."

"Ooh, how romantic," the woman sighed.

Thankful Warren was able to charm the woman and cover up her goof, Clarissa sent up a silent thank you as they returned to the bike and once again went roaring down the road.

Soon she could smell the ocean and she breathed in deep. It was salty and fresh and she liked the scent very much. Wherever he was taking her, the ocean and beach were near and she couldn't wait to see it.

They crossed the bridge to Marco Island and then Warren found a building to park behind that had no lights in front or in back. "We'll walk from here," he said. "No one should see the bike here." They got off and he started to unload the things they needed.

"Where are we going?" Clarissa asked as she pulled the coin belt out of the bag.

"Somewhere we can camp tonight."

Clarissa wrapped the belt around her waist.

"You and that coin belt." He shook his head.

"My good luck. It kept me alive with Mr. Peason, and then you found me, and now here we are. It smells like the ocean here, and I bet we are near the beach. See my good luck?"

"I'm glad you having it kept something worse from happening."

"Me too."

It was dark as they walked, but Clarissa could hear the roar of the waves nearby as they crossed one street and got nearer to what she was sure was a beach.

"You said you wanted to go to the beach."

"Oh, yes," she said. "I can hear it. It's lovely." She could hardly contain her excitement and then they were there. Standing with the sand stretching down to the water's edge and the waves rolling in and out.

He picked a spot, and flicking on his flashlight set about putting up the tent. First, he staked out the area he wanted to pitch the tent, and then about two feet away from where one of the tent stakes would go, he dug a hole in the sand. Handing her a plastic shopping bag and a plastic cup, he said, "Here, fill this with sand, all the way to the top."

She used the plastic cup to start filling the bag. When it was full she said, "Now what?"

He held out another one toward her. "Now this one."

They continued until he'd dug four holes in the sand and she'd filled four bags. Then he set up the tent and tied it down to the sand bags. Taking the cup, he got water and wet the bags to make them heavier. "That should do it," he said. "Now we'll need to leave our shoes outside and be careful not to get sand everywhere. It's not the most comfortable thing sleeping on sand and it gets into everything if you let it." He turned and looked at her. "Well, what do you think?"

"Oh, Warren," she breathed. "I think it's wonderful." She looked up at the night sky with the stars above and then back to the ocean. "It's marvelous."

"You wanted to go to the beach." He smiled. "I'm glad I could make that wish come true."

"I never dreamed of anything like this." She sighed. "It's so romantic."

"It is," he said with a smile. "I wanted to give you something good. Before I take you to the place where you'll be staying."

"The place where I'll be staying…" She didn't like the sound of that.

"Yes. We haven't really had a chance to talk, because there hasn't been time. I wanted to find a place where we could talk. They'll expect us to be on the run, not camping on a beach. Often the best way to avoid a bad guy is to do something unpredictable and unexpected."

"That's interesting. I wouldn't have thought of that."

"You want the bad guy to be unable to predict your next move. It can buy you time and help you to get away."

She nodded. "Makes sense."

He sat on the sand and took off his boots and she sat beside him. "It's peaceful here. I haven't had that since I walked into the shuttle station. Thank you."

"You're welcome." He pulled off his socks.

She took off her shoes and sunk her toes into the sand and then wiggled them and giggled. "This feels good." She looked up at him. "I hope the place I'll be staying is near here."

"It's in Florida, but not on a beach. Nor should you try to come here without me. You'll need to stay in the camp to avoid detection. But I can bring you here when I come to visit."

"So, you're not staying with me."

"Not once you're safe there. No."

"I knew you'd leave once I was safe again. I knew you wouldn't stay and I'd probably never see you again."

Cupping her jaw with his hand, he turned her face to look into her eyes. "I will see you again. I'm not abandoning you."

Her eyes widened.

He'd just touched on her one big fear since she'd met him. One that had grown the more time she spent with him. The more she depended on him. The more attached she was to him. He'd just dared to name her one big fear and to address it.

"Thank you," she whispered.

"Darling," he said. "I'm here with you because I want to be with you, not just because I need to be to protect you. You've never been just a job to me. From the moment I saw you, when I first saw you in that lounge, I thought of kissing you."

"Oh." She caught her breath as his words surprised her and then she let them sink in.

He watched her in silence, his eyes taking in everything.

Then her words came rushing back and there was so much she wanted to say that they came out in a rush. "Why can't I stay with you? I feel safe with you."

"Because you wouldn't be safe where I'm going and I need you to be safe."

"I'll do anything you tell me to do. I just want to stay with you. Please?"

He shook his head. "No. I can't do my job if I have to worry about keeping you safe."

"You said where you're going I won't be safe. That means you won't be safe either. You're going to do something dangerous."

Warren just looked at her and shrugged.

"The work you do. Is it always dangerous?"

"Yes. Life is dangerous."

"It is. I had no idea how much that was true."

"You just never saw it before."

"I was too busy dancing. Blinded by the sparkly things and the stage lights."

"But that's over now."

"Yes. I don't want to go onto a stage any more. Any stage."

"Good. That wouldn't be safe for you."

"No, it wouldn't. And I don't want that kind of attention any more. Though I still like to dance and I'd dance for you."

Warren smiled but didn't answer.

"Would you like me to dance for you?"

"Maybe one day." He threaded his fingers through the hair at the back of her neck and looked into her eyes. "I'd rather you kiss me."

She smiled, leaned forward and did just that. Kissing beneath the stars was the most romantic thing she'd ever done. The sound of the waves and the glow of the moon and the taste and feel of his lips upon hers were memories she would keep with her forever when he was gone.

Warren was like no man she'd ever been with before. He cared about her safety and about her happiness. And the way he kissed, tender and giving, made her senses reel. She could've stayed here on this beach kissing him forever.

He finally pulled away and smiled at her.

She smiled back, feeling warm and flushed with a happy glow.

"I like kissing you." His words rolled over her as his eyes drank her image in.

"I like kissing you too." Her words came out breathless.

"Before we get too carried away, I want to tell you about where we're going. The camp where you'll be staying"

"Yes." She wanted to know and he was finally ready to talk about it. "Where is this camp you're taking me to?"

"More importantly, what is it," he corrected her. "There's a camp hidden in a swampy area of Florida where other herbalists live."

"There is?" Her eyes widened.

"Yes. So, you'll be around others who share your interests and who will be excited for you to help them with their work. They're already excited to learn that Deep Nest discovered your herbs and they're looking forward to meeting you. How does that sound to you?"

"That sounds wonderful," she said hugging her legs and looking out at the ocean. "Kind of like my life is moving from a nightmare into a happy dream."

"Good."

She turned to him again. "Will I be able to work with the heirloom seeds from my aunt?"

"Yes, with those and with others. There are several camps in different states, and their network shares seedlings and plants when they can smuggle them across and into the camp. The idea is to have some of each variety and spread them around. If one of the camps is discovered, the seed varieties are not wiped out."

"I'm glad. Yes, I'd like to work with them."

"I thought you would, and was pretty sure of your answer, but it still needed to be your choice. So, we're agreed then? I'll take you there tomorrow."

"Yes, we're agreed. I'm looking forward to it. And you're sure I'll be safe there?"

"It is the safest of the camps. The hardest to find. Between the swampland, the alligators and the camp guards, this camp is incredibly hard to break into, and unlikely to be accidentally discovered. I can't think of a better place for you."

"Good." She smiled, using his word. There was something about the way he said it and something about his voice. His favorite word was rapidly becoming her favorite as well.

Appearing pleased, he seemed more settled and relaxed than he had since she'd known him. He watched the surf move in and out along with her in companionable silence and they enjoyed the sight and sounds together.

Then, unable to hold back the question that had hovered even as she rested there with him, she said, "When will you come back to visit?"

"In between missions." His gaze returned to hers. "I'll check on you when I can, but I won't be able to say when, and messages could be delayed or even difficult. I am often...out of touch."

"I see." She cleared her throat and looked back at the stunning view. "Well, then I'll just be surprised and happy to see you." This was more than what she'd thought she'd have. If they were beginning a relationship, she'd just have to be happy with that. Soon he'd leave, and she'd be alone in a place she'd never been, with people she didn't yet know. "I don't suppose I'd be allowed to talk to any of my dance sisters. To let them know I'm okay. I'd like to at least be able to check in with Leila. So, she won't worry."

"No," he said. "Sorry sweetheart. For now, they can't know anything about you, only that you've disappeared. If everything were to change, well we are working for that day."

She nodded. "Okay. They'll worry. Especially Leila. And if they think I'm dead they will grieve. I don't like knowing her heart will be hurting because of me."

"It's the way it has to be."

"I understand. I just wish it were different."

"I do too." His fingers threaded through hers and they held hands for a while, until she began to get sleepy, her eyes drifting down. "Come on, sweetheart," his voice woke her enough she sat up straighter. "Time for bed." He stood and pulled her to her feet. "You're exhausted." He moved toward the tent and opened the flap. "My lady," he said.

127

"Why, thank you." She smiled as she entered the tent. He followed and closed the flap behind him, zipping it closed.

Clarissa knelt and untied the hip scarf from around her waist. The coins jangled as she took it off and a little bit of sand fell from it. After gently folding it, she placed it in the corner of the tent where it would be out of the way. She wanted it near her.

"Tell me the significance of that coin belt, Clarissa." His voice was strong and intimate.

"It was my mother's."

"Ah," he said. "I see."

"She only wore it once—before she was killed."

"Was she wearing it when…" his voice came gentle now.

"No, not that day. She never wore a coin belt or hip scarf in a show, she was a stripper not a belly dancer."

"What's the difference between a hip scarf and a coin belt?"

"Well a hip scarf might not have coins. A coin belt will."

"So, yours is a coin belt."

"Well, it's a hip scarf with coins. It's been called both. Honestly, I'm not sure of the difference. Someone might've known at some time, but none of my teachers explained it. Belly dance in the U.S. is a mishmash of so many styles from different countries and there's history to those original dances, but here we tend to do our own thing. The modern styles are a blend of many kinds of dances."

"I see."

"I didn't really have formal teachers. Belly dancing was something mother did at home. She and her friend and sometimes roommate, Jannah. I watched their moves when I was little and then I'd try to copy them. I grew up around dancers and at home they danced for fun. It was just part of their lifestyle. But after I went to live with my aunt on the farm, there was no more dancing. It wasn't allowed. Then Jannah showed up out of the blue and gave the coin belt to me on my eighteenth birthday, saying I ought to have something of my mother's. It's the only thing I have of hers."

"You about drove me crazy with that bright, noisy coin belt. I was trying to keep you safe."

"I know. You were quite exasperated with me."

"Yes, I was. But I understand why you're so attached to it now. What's the good luck about?"

"It was in my bag when I got my first apartment and I wore it when I got my first job as a dancer. It just kept bringing me luck and helping me to be independent. I didn't want to be a farmer. I wanted to live in the city and be away from the rules of my aunt. When I moved off the farm, I tried to find Jannah, but she'd moved away and no one knew where she'd gone. Mother's hip scarf has always brought me luck, more times than I can list, and it's the only thing I have left that was hers. When I wrap her hip scarf around me, I feel like she's near."

"I understand." His voice was soothing and low, and it stirred something deep within her. "To leave it behind would be like losing part of your mother."

129

"Yes." She nodded in the dark. "It really does bring me good luck. Even now, with bad things happening. If I hadn't had it with me when that man kidnapped me, things would've gone worse. I'd have been as bad off as those other women and he would've sold me already, before you found me. Then you might never have found me."

"That was good thinking." He cupped her cheek. "I was worried something had happened to you. But Clarissa," he waited until she looked into his eyes and then emphasized his next words, "I would have found you."

She smiled at him, eyes shining. "I believe you." She nodded. "You would have." She leaned into his hand, enjoying the warmth.

"You're chilled," he said, his voice edged with concern.

"And you're warm," she said.

"I can warm you up."

She thought about that and about how he'd left her before with no note. Though he claimed he'd only gone for donuts and coffee. He should've woken her up if he wasn't leaving a note. Though she wanted to trust his words now and trust where their relationship was going, as every part of her heart was crying out for that, there was still that one very real and very recent event which she hadn't gotten over yet. It still felt as if he'd left her. Because he had. "Are you going to run off in the morning if I let you warm me up?"

"No." He gave her a look like he couldn't believe she was asking the question. But she might as well ask now and put it out there, so she knew what she was dealing with.

"I didn't run off, I was getting coffee."

"I don't need you to bring me coffee. I don't even drink coffee."

"Well I do drink coffee, and I need it in the morning. But I won't leave to get it next time without waking you first. Okay?"

Watching him, she decided she would trust him. *Trust is always a leap, even when you thought surely you can trust a man. That is when they blind-sided you.*

"Okay." She nodded. "Then I suppose I can let you warm me up tonight."

He watched and listened without answering, though she'd have bet he was thinking, good. Then the word came, in a soft whisper. "Good."

Tingles ran up her spine and she longed for him to kiss her. "I hope you'll warm me up, all over." If they were only going to have tonight before he rode off again, she was going to ask for what she wanted. For everything she wanted.

He gave her a deep smile and then took her hand. "I want to make love to you beneath the stars."

She caught her breath. He'd found one of her favorite fantasies without asking her what they were. "I've never made love on a beach. I'd love that. It sounds so romantic."

"Then come on," he said, tugging on her hand. "Let's make it happen.

He kissed the inside of her wrist where her pulse was jumping. He gazed into her eyes searching.

Fear and trust warred with each other there and he

was reading her, seeing into her as his eyes searched, catching every nuance. It was as if he was taking inventory and making love to her with his eyes before kissing her again and it made her feel laid wide open because she was letting him see inside. Something she never did when she had to perform in bed, naked. It made her feel new again, like she'd never been with anyone, because she'd never let any man in so close, to see her every emotion.

Trusting, leaping, her last thought was this. *I'll trust him one more time. And if all we have is tonight, that will be enough. At least we'll have tonight before he rides off.* And with that, she pushed her thoughts aside, and opened her arms and her heart wide open to him. Then she followed him out of the tent to stand beneath the stars.

He kissed her one on the lips and then said, "Stay right here."

She stood while he went back into the tent for the blanket and hadn't moved when he came back with it. He kissed her on the lips again and then he spread the blanket upon the sand. "This will keep the sand out when we make love."

"I feel like I'm dreaming,," Clarissa said. "I can't believe we're here at the beach, all alone. There's not a person in sight. It's been one of my dreams, to make love on a on a beach."

He sat on the blanket and patted the spot next to him. She sat beside him and then leaned back on her elbows. They watched the stars for a while and then he leaned over and kissed her.

Relaxing into the kiss she drifted down and down onto the blanket. His kisses sent her to into a half awake half daydream state where she floated until he suddenly stopped and rolled her over quickly until she was on top of him, taking her by surprise. She could feel his hard length beneath her and knew how much he wanted her. Teasing him with a little rock of her hips she said, "I've been thinking about this every time we ride that Harley."

He grasped her hips and guiding her to rock some more said, "This would be so much better if you were naked."

"I can get naked pretty fast." She stood quickly and began peeling off her clothes.

"Race you," he said and the race was on.

The moment they were both naked he got back on the blanket and laying back he pulled her close and said, "Ride me."

"I'm surprised you want me to be on top our first time together."

"You're in charge tonight, babe. Do with me whatever you want."

Looking at his strong well-muscled body she wasn't sure where to start so she bent down to kiss him and then he pulled her closer saying "You're too far away. Straddle me."

She did, noting that this tough SEAL was commanding her from beneath despite him telling her that she was in charge. She wondered what he'd do if she took charge back. Feeling a burst of confidence, which came out of nowhere she said, "Straddle you? I want to ride you, Mr."

"Then ride."

And with that she mounted him slow, sinking down as his hard length drove up inside of her. Going slowly until he was all the way in, she closed her eyes and stayed still for a moment and then started to move her hips, slow and rhythmic. "That's it baby," he said.

He let her rock for a while before he finally gripped her hips. "Show me what these belly dancing hips can do now."

"Oh, I will show you, Mr."

"Too much talk," he said. "Ride."

She began to move her hips in slow circles.

His hands urged her to move faster. "Yes, baby, that's it," he said.

Faster and faster she rocked until she was soon feeling a wave begin inside of her as she heard the waves crashing behind them. The wave rising and then crashing and then another rising again, until she crashed with a shudder. Then he came, hard and fast, as if he'd held out for the last possible moment for her to be satisfied. Just as she was finishing that final wave he'd joined her and then they were both sated. Panting she sat atop him as a sudden languor came over her and her eyelids felt heavy. The breeze on her back felt cool and she shivered slightly.

Come here," he said and he pulled her down close to be held. His warm arms wrapped around her and she nestled in. He kissed her temple. "I like the way you ride," he said.

"I liked riding you," she said. "And making love on the beach."

"I liked it too." After a moment, he rolled her over.

"I feel exposed here on the beach. Anyone could

see us."

"It didn't bother you before."

"You're right, it didn't. I wasn't thinking about other people."

"We can go into the tent if you'd like."

"Yes, I'd like to do that."

He sat up and held out his and. "Come on then."

She put her hand in his and they rose together.

Once he had them zipped into their tent, he laid back down and reached for her. "Come here, baby. I'll put you to sleep."

Wondering just how he'd do that, she curled up next to him and he wrapped one arm around her. With the other he stroked her long silky hair and within minutes she was asleep.

* * * *

In her dream, they were chasing her. A gang of men in orange shoes and a woman in a purple turban screaming, "Get her!" She ran and ran, but she couldn't lose them and Warren was nowhere to be found. She called and called for him, but she was on her own. He wasn't coming. She was all alone. Just when one of them grabbed her arm and she screamed, she felt herself being gently shaken awake.

"Clarissa, baby, wake up. It's just a dream. You're safe."

Shaking, she looked up at him and wanted to crawl into his arms and be held forever. Without another word, he pulled her close.

135

"They were chasing me. The woman in the purple turban and lots of men. They all wore orange shoes. They were chasing me, they were everywhere, and I couldn't find you."

"It's over. I'm right here. There's just you and me here, and the ocean."

When the remnants of the nightmare faded away, she whispered, "Thank you."

"Hush. You don't need to thank me for this." He kissed her forehead. "Listen to the waves and I'll hold you. Go to sleep now."

She slept with the waves on the beach as her lullaby and Warren's arms around her.

In the morning, she woke to find him watching her, his eyes soft and tender. "Morning, sweetheart. I hope you slept better."

"Once you were holding me, I did."

"Have you been having bad dreams like that often?"

"I didn't dream at all when Mr. Peason had me locked up. I slept very lightly. Every sound would wake me. I ought to be sleeping like a baby as tired as I am."

"You will. You've been through a lot and there's a lot to process."

"I guess so."

"Hungry?"

"Yes."

"Good. Let's break camp and get some breakfast.

We need to break the tent down and get on the road before more people are up and come nosing around."

"Okay."

They hurried to dress and then broke the tent down. Soon everything was stowed back on the bike and they were off in search of a hot breakfast.

****

The Florida heat beat down as they rode the airboat through the Everglades. Clarissa brushed the hair off her face and tried to ignore the sweat rolling down her back as she listened to the noise of the big airplane engine that drove the boat through the swamp. Partly it was the humidity and partly nerves making her sweat. Getting here had felt like such a cloak and dagger movie and they still weren't at the camp yet.

Warren wasn't kidding when he'd said the camp wasn't easy to get to. He'd stowed the Harley at a friend's house and the friend had given them a ride to a tourist place several miles away that took visitors on airboat rides. Warren paid for a private ride and they'd climbed on board the airboat. At first, it was fun. Their Native American guide started the boat and soon the big windy motor in back was pushing them along.

The water was brown and in places where the trees reflected on the water, green. Tree trunks with strange roots predominated, and trees hung low or stood high, often with a bird perched atop. She watched as a white crane atop a tree stump opened its wings, took off and caught her breath at the beauty of it. "Did you see that?" she asked Warren. As she turned to him she realized he'd been watching her. "Isn't it beautiful?"

"Yes, beautiful" he said with a smile, taking his finger, and pulling the strands of hair in her eyes away.

She turned back to watch, afraid to miss something.

All the birds and reptiles they passed were showing her a part of the U.S. she'd never seen before. With the tall sawgrasses and the animals hiding, this did seem like a good part of the country to hide in. But once the boat pulled up to a muddy embankment, Warren said, "We'll be getting off here."

"Oh. Okay." Clarissa was surprised as it looked as if no one had ever set foot here. Looking for any trace of men having been on the bank, she saw nothing. "Has anyone ever landed here before?"

"Many times."

Knowing they'd be getting off here, she started to get nervous. Here the trees were tall, moss hung down low and there was no path she could see ahead of them.

"Watch the sawgrass," their guide said. "It will cut you." It was the only time the silent man had addressed her.

"Oh," Clarissa said. "Yes, thank you."

The guide nodded, silent.

They stepped out of the boat onto the muddy bank.

"Thanks." Warren slipped the guide money and said, "We were never here."

The guide nodded as if expecting that and then started the boat without another glance at the two of them. An alligator could have eaten them right now and no one would ever know. She gave a nervous shiver.

Warren took her by the hand and said, "Come on.

138

Nothing to be afraid of. I've got you."

Forcing away her thoughts of alligators and crocs and other crawling things that might be in the vegetation they were moving into, she clung to his hand and followed him into the swampy trees.

Just as they stepped into the vegetation, a dark black snake with light bands slithered fast across the ground in front of them.

Clarissa screamed and clung onto Warren.

"I got you, baby." His arm wrapped around her. "It's all right. We just startled it."

"Snakes! There are snakes in there! I'm not going in there!"

"It's okay. That's just a small king snake. They're the good snakes."

"There are no good snakes!"

Patiently, he held onto her and kept explaining in a firm, calm voice. "The good snakes eat the bad snakes. They're more afraid of us. Once they hear us coming…"

"Nooo. I can't. I just can't." She hung onto his arm crying and shaking her head. "They are not more afraid of us. Nooo, I can't go in there."

"We have to. You're going to be okay. It's gone. Take a deep breath."

She took a deep breath and then her voice dropped to a whisper. "I'm afraid of snakes. I can't go in there."

"Nothing bad is going to happen to you. I'm right here." He gave her a squeeze and then let go and reached for her hand. "Come on. We have no other choice. The boat is gone. There's no going back."

With a worried frown, she clung to his hand and followed him in.

About a half hour later, they came to a wire fence that held a red danger sign. Taking the sign, he flipped it over, so it faced the other way. "Now, we wait," he said.

"What does the sign mean?" she whispered.

"No need to whisper," he said. "It's like a keep out sign. This is an area where two men keep a sort of hunting cabin and flipping the sign over keeps us from getting shot at."

"Goodness. I'm glad you knew to flip it over."

"Oh, they'd have watched us first to see what we did. Only someone persistent enough to keep going would get shot at."

"I'm almost afraid to ask, but what are they hunting?"

"Gators, snakes, sometimes men."

"Are there gators and snakes in there?"

"No more so than the area we just walked through."

"Oh." She shivered. "Why'd you have to tell me that?"

"Did you see any gators or snakes on the way here once we were off the boat?"

"N…no." She still couldn't get it out of her mind

"You're fine, sweetheart. Nothing is going to hurt

you." He turned his head. "Here he comes now."

"What do you two want?" A dark haired bearded man with broad shoulders wearing a hat down low over his eyes stepped within sight of the fence, a shotgun in his hands pointing straight at them.

Clarissa jumped and held onto Warren's arm, her heart racing. The man looked crazy and like he would shoot them at any moment.

CHAPTER NINE

Warren placed his hand on hers and calmly stated, "Looking for a goldfinch nest."

The bearded man squinted at Warren for a moment then looked at Clarissa and spat. "That the goldfinch?"

"Yes," Warren said.

"Chirp, chirp," Clarissa blurted out, her nerves getting the best of her. "Just call me birdie."

The side of the bearded man's mouth twitched in a grin. Then he cleared his throat. "Come on." He went down the fence a little further and unlocked a padlock, then swung the gate open.

Once Clarissa and Warren were through, he swung it shut and locked it again. He looked down at her slim legs and wet, muddy feet. "Ya need rain boots, little birdie."

She glanced at her sodden shoes and feet. "Yes, though I suppose it doesn't matter now."

"Might have a pair to fit ya."

They followed him to a wooden cabin in a small clearing. Traps and canoes sat to one side of it. Cages on the other. Clarissa was glad the cages were empty and also glad Warren was holding her hand again.

"Wait here," the man said and he stomped up the steps and into the cabin.

They stood waiting and soon he emerged with a pair of men's boots and a pail of water. "Here, ya want to wash them legs and feet first." He held the water pail out to her and she took it from him and sat on the steps. He plunked the boots down beside her. "Smallest pair I have."

The boots were going to be big on her, as they were men's rain boots, but she'd make do. She picked up one foot to step forward and the big boot slid around and down her foot. She took a step and tried to walk but almost fell.

"It would be better if you shuffle walked," Warren said. "They're not going to stay on otherwise."

She tried a shuffle walk and felt awkward and clumsy. It would be slow going if she had to walk like that.

"Oh, hell that won't do. Hang on," the hunter said and he went back into the cabin. Then he returned with a roll of black duct tape. Wrapping it around the top of one boot to make it fit her calf, he said, "This oughta help to keep 'em on and keep stuff out."

"Keep stuff out?" Her voice squeaked a bit as she looked around, imagining what he might mean by stuff. Was it creepy crawlers or mud or something nasty? She still hadn't gotten over the sight of that slithering, wiggling snake crossing their path and she shivered.

He taped around the other boot and then said, "Hold out your arms."

She held out her arms and he pulled a bottle of bug spray out of one pocket and started spraying her down.

Coughing, she said, "Do you have to put so much on?"

"Ya can wash it off when ya get to camp, but we got to get ya there first. Bugs will feast on a little birdie like you if we let 'em."

Coughing again, she placed one hand over her nose and tried not to breathe the bug stuff.

When he was done, he handed the can to Warren who sprayed himself quickly and was done.

"All right," the hunter said, tossing the can onto the porch of the cabin, and picking up his gun. "Come with me." He led them past the cabin and into the deep vegetation.

They walked in silence for what seemed like a long time to Clarissa. She followed behind the hunter and Warren came behind her. He steadied her by taking hold of her arm when she tripped, which was more often than she liked.

If only they would reach the camp soon. She couldn't help looking left and right as she imagined alligators or snakes coming out of the vegetation toward them.

As it began to get darker both men turned on flashlights. Clarissa said, "How much longer?"

"Thirty minutes, maybe longer, depending on how fast you go," their guide replied.

"Sorry I'm so slow and clumsy." Her feet and legs were tired from the too big boots and she wished they would hurry up and get there. She'd walk faster if she weren't so tired.

How far have we walked anyway? Maybe it is better not to

ask right now. That is a sit down and ask after we get there kind of question.

"Ya got to get some boots that fit ya."

And just where was she supposed to do that? Wasn't like there were stores anywhere. It wasn't something she wanted to think about, how cut off they were. So, she didn't reply, but instead concentrated on walking without tripping.

"Just keep moving, goldfinch," Warren said in an encouraging tone. "You're doing fine. We'll be there soon."

His voice steadied her and helped her to press on, when what she really wanted to do was to stop, sit down and rest.

At last, they reached a place where the vegetation wasn't as heavy. People had cleared it, and a man stepped out from behind a tree and said, "Halt."

All three of them stopped. Then the man said, "That you, Jim?"

"Yep," the hunter replied.

So, we finally get his name, Clarissa thought. *But he doesn't really have ours.* The thought that he couldn't give away names he didn't know occurred to her and she wondered what would happen if the people after her found Jim. He didn't seem like the type to easily be found or to be captured. More than likely, he'd slip away into the swamp like some gator.

"Got a songbird to deliver," he said, nodding toward her.

"Goldfinch, we've been expecting you," the other

man said. "Thanks, Jim."

Without replying Jim turned and was gone. She turned to look after him, but all she saw was waving vegetation and the blackness of night.

"Follow me," the man said. "Brandon has been driving everyone nuts preparing and pacing. He'll be glad to know you made it."

"Who is Brandon?" she asked.

"One of the herbalists you'll be working with. He's very enthusiastic."

"I'm only staying two nights," Warren said. "Have any messages or packages ready before I go and I'll take them."

"I'll spread the word."

They followed him to the outskirts of the camp, which consisted of several cabins, a greenhouse, and a covered picnic area with a few grills. A man with a green lizard on a yellow T-shirt hurried up to them and Clarissa paused and took a step back, his T-shirt reminding her of the Lounging Lizard on top of the bar she'd danced at.

Warren placed his hand on her lower back, both to steady and reassure her, and marking his territory in the way that men do, for the eager man approaching them and anyone else who might be watching.

"Hello! Welcome! I'm so glad you're here!" Brandon first shook her hand and then Warren's. "We're all looking forward to meeting you."

"Thank you. I'm …" she hesitated.

"You are goldfinch also known as… well we can

146

use our real names here." He winked. "Though goldfinch is a pretty name. It suits you."

"Thank you. I, I'm Clarissa Heat and this is Warren." She gestured to him.

"Good to meet you both. Let me show you around," Brandon said. "The first thing you'll want to see are the herb beds. We're having great success with them and with cultivating the seeds to share with the other herbalists in the country."

"How do you share the seeds with them?" Warren asked.

"One of us travels to them, kind of like Johnny Appleseed. He's been going around the country, quietly sharing the seeds, he goes by the name of Cody Vale."

"Interesting."

"It really is," Brandon's excitement was contagious and Clarissa smiled, his enthusiasm boosting her up.

"I've been growing on my own for so long, it's exciting to meet others who are growing from seeds." She smiled. "I'm excited to be able to pass along my aunt's herbs. I've been all alone with this."

"You haven't known anyone else who grows herbs?" He seemed surprised.

"Just my aunt, but she passed years ago. I never knew anyone else grew them, until now."

"So, I'm your first?" Brandon's face lit up while Warren frowned. "Your first herbalist friend?"

"Why, yes, yes you are," Clarissa said.

"Well, I'm not the only one here. There are several

others. There's Hachi and Suwanee, they're both Seminole Indians and they have cabin two, over there." He pointed to the cabin. "Then Vivaan and Prisha Patel, they are from India and are in cabin three to the right of cabin two. Cabin four is Red's. He doesn't like to be bothered, so don't knock on his door. Cabin one is mine and you're in cabin five. Everyone is excited to meet you. Just wait till you meet them! You'll have a whole new family."

She smiled at the thought. "I'd like that. I've been alone with this for so long."

"You're not alone anymore," Warren reminded her.

She turned to him and reached for his hand. "Thank you for bringing me here. It's perfect."

Seeing how happy she was, he couldn't help but smile. "You're welcome."

Brandon drew their attention back and picked up his pace. "Cabins are this way. I'm sure you'll want to get settled in and wash up." They followed him until they reached a cabin on the far end. "This will be your cabin. Go on in."

Warren placed his hand on the small of Clarissa's back and nudged her forward.

So, this was to be her new home. It was tiny, with just enough room for a cot, a folding chair, a folding table, a cooler, and a plastic tub in the corner to store things in.

From outside, Brandon spoke again. "You have to just think of this like camping; store your clothes in the tub to keep them dry and keep the bugs out and store food and drinks in the cooler. There's a sleeping bag and pillow in the tub right now. So, you have everything you need to get started."

"It's safer than camping in a tent when storms come." Warren said. "Do you evacuate for hurricanes?"

"We do, as needed," Brandon said. "We can go mobile pretty quickly."

"I wouldn't know where to go," Clarissa said.

"We'll look after you," Brandon said. "Part of the family, remember?"

Clarissa nodded. *This family stuff is going to take a little getting used to.*

"Go ahead and stow your stuff and then we'll move on to the greenhouse."

"Is there a…um, toilet anywhere?"

"Oh, yes, of course. Toilets, showers, and even hot water. Now, it's a little bit rough. You have to turn it on to heat the water before you shower. And the toilet is more like an outhouse. But it's an improvement on what we did have."

They walked toward a small wooden outhouse and the men waited while Clarissa used the facilities. She could hear them outside talking.

"What can you tell me about the security measures here?" Warren asked.

"Oh, I let the guards handle all that," Brandon said. "You'll have to talk to them."

She came out and handed her flashlight back to Brandon.

149

"I'll let you keep this one when we get back to your house," he said. "I have others."

"Thank you," she said. "I didn't come here with much."

"Whatever you need, just let me know and I'll see if we have it." Brandon nodded. "If not, we'll get it sent in."

"Great," she said.

"Now, this tent," he pointed the flashlight at it. "Is the shower tent." They walked closer until they stood outside of it. A sign hanging outside read unoccupied. He reached for it and flipped it over.

"Turn the sign to occupied, unless you want company," he said with a laugh. Shining the light into the tent he motioned for them to step inside.

In the middle of the tent were plastic grates like the old-fashioned milk crates in the antique stores. Clarissa was glad she wouldn't have to stand in mud in flip-flops when she showered. This way she could wash the bottoms of her feet, dry them, and put shoes on.

Brandon drew her attention by pointing to a metal pot. "First you boil the water in this big pot, then you pour it in the reservoir with the cold water to warm it up. Now, it only holds fifteen gallons, so you can't dilly dally in there. You have to wet yourself, turn it off, soap up and then turn it on again to rinse. There's a peg for your towel, make sure it's on there good or it will fall in the mud."

Clarissa had never been camping before the night on the beach with Warren, so she was glad Brandon was showing her how everything worked instead of leaving her to figure it out on her own. She wondered how fast she'd have to shower to wash herself and her long hair. The hair Warren had asked her to cut. She glanced at him and saw him watching her quietly in the dark tent.

Brandon swept the flashlight back to the entrance, capturing her attention again. "Ladies first."

"Thank you." Clarissa stepped out. "I didn't bring a towel and washcloth."

"Oh, I can get you a towel. Do you need shampoo? Prisha makes her own shampoo and soaps and they're lavender scented."

"That sounds wonderful."

"She likes making soaps and shampoos. So much better for you than the store bought."

"Oh yes, they would be."

Warren's hand wrapped around hers as they walked, Clarissa getting caught up in chatter with the other herbalist about herbal soaps, cleaning supplies and other things they could make here. His quiet presence beside her calmed her in a way she could not have described.

* * * *

Watching Clarissa bloom as she talked to the other herbalist, Warren saw a whole new side of the woman who had planted a seed in his heart. She held a beautiful glow, one that needed no makeup or fancy clothes. One that was perhaps more hidden by those things. This glow of happiness reassured him she would be fine here. More than fine and he had no more misgivings about leaving her here. Here she'd be safe and more than safe, she'd thrive doing something she loved. Good.

Not so good was the overeager man talking to her now. *Brandon. He was entirely too eager.*

Warren wished he'd had more time with Clarissa. One night on the beach together was a good start, but more time would have been better. The problem was, time was not something he had much of. He was already stretching it to stay one extra day instead of leaving tomorrow. They had a mission and the guys were waiting on him.

Well, he'd make the most of the time he and Clarissa did have. He gave her hand a squeeze and waited for the man to quit chattering to her now that they'd reached her cabin. Soon they'd be alone.

"Warren," Brandon finally turned his attention away from Clarissa. "You can bunk down in my cabin. I have a spare cot."

"Clarissa and I have a lot to talk about before I leave."

Brandon's eyebrows lifted with surprise. "Oh. I see." He was quiet for the longest stretch since he'd said hello.

"Can you bring the cot over here?" Clarissa turned her shining eyes to Brandon and she smiled. "He can stay with me."

"Oh. Yes. Of course."

Warren slid his arm around Clarissa's waist. "Good."

* * * *

Clarissa wished Warren didn't have to leave. Their time together had flown much too fast. Now the sun was up, the birds were singing and he sat on the cot lacing up his boots.

"I wish you could stay another day."

"I do too, sweetheart." He tied off the last lace and then walked over to her. She stood and then he pulled her close and gave her a long kiss.

They'd talked about how he had to leave at first light. Then both had stayed awake most of the night, making love to each other, kissing, and touching as if they'd never see each other again. Neither of them wanted to sleep. She touched the corner of his tired eyes with her fingertips and said, "You're tired. I wish you weren't so tired."

"I'm fine. Don't worry. I'll be fine."

"If there's a way for you to let me know you're all right…"

"We've talked about this."

"I know. We can't communicate the regular ways."

"Sweetheart, I don't want you expecting messages and waiting for them. That's not a good way. If I get one through it will be a surprise."

"I guess that will have to be enough."

"Yes, it will."

"Okay," she sighed. "I can do that."

"Good."

She grinned. "You know I can't hear that word without thinking of you."

His whole face smiled and though he didn't say it, she knew he was thinking the word good.

Then he wrapped his arms around her, pulled her close and kissed her deep and long, letting her know how much he desired her. She gave herself completely into the kiss, letting him know how much she also desired him, and how much she would miss him. When he finally broke the kiss, they both caught their breath and he said, "It's time."

"I know." She held back the rest of the words she could have said. Of how she wished he didn't have to go, of how much she would miss him. She pushed all that aside, to show him she would be strong as he needed her to be and not clingy.

"Stay here. I know you don't like the edges of the camp."

She really didn't, with the snakes and God knew what else out there. She eyed the edge of the vegetation and said, "Okay."

"Good." He kissed her forehead and then winked at her and suddenly he was out the door and moving away toward the guarded edges of the camp before she even had a chance to tear up.

Alone in her cabin, standing in the doorway, she watched him go.

She'd get used to being alone. She'd lived alone before. It wasn't like she hadn't ever been alone before. This was just new. She had a whole lot of new to get used to, but thanks to Warren she was now safe and among her own kind. It would be exciting to work with the seeds and grow herbs again. This was important work they were doing. This would be her new home and he really had found the best place for her to hide and thrive. She told herself all this as she watched him walk away. And then he walked into the rainy mists and was gone.

Realization settled over her, maybe the change of scenery wasn't what she needed. Maybe what she needed was Warren. *Maybe all that matters is who you are with, not where you are.*

And in that moment, she wanted him back.

She looked around at the scene in front of her, at the small cabins surrounding hers, at the swampy trees, the rain, and the mists from all the wetness. She'd wanted a change of scenery more than anything and now that she had it, she wasn't so sure. Slowly she turned and walked back into the one room cabin, which was her new home.

She plopped on her cot. *How gloomy it is in here.*

There was nothing about it that seemed homey to her. This was just a place to sleep. A place to keep her things. Not a home. Dark from the gloomy rain, the mood of the room and her mood needed to be lifted.

She turned on the flashlight Brandon had given her and placed it on the bed facing out to light up the room, which helped some, but didn't alleviate the gloom. Taking her red hip scarf from its storage place, she hung it from one nail on the wall to another nail. It brightened up the place as the red fabric and gold coins caught the light and said, a belly dancer lives here.

Briefly, she wondered how her dance sisters were, and if any of them missed her. Leila would have when she didn't check in with her. Though it might take some time as they all thought she'd flown to the Caribbean for her vacation. Her time with the troupe seemed from another life long ago, so much had happened since.

There would be no dancing here, no stages to perform on, no putting on a show for anyone. *Did they even have mirrors?* She hadn't seen one. There was no need for makeup, or dance clothes or shoes or any of those fancy, girly things she used to love so much. She'd always been girly, not so much a tomboy. This camp was going to take some getting used to but at least she'd have her herbs to work with, and maybe she would find other things to make her little cabin feel more like a home. She thought about all the pretty things she had at her home. All the things she had just walked away from because she'd had no other choice. It was sad to have to do that, but the main thing was, she'd be safe here.

She moved to the doorway and stared out the open door at the rain, trying not to let the gloom get to her.

Looking back over her shoulder at the cheerful coin belt, seeing how it claimed her space, marking the small cabin as hers and giving it personality, she was cheered by the red and gold and the memories that came with the coin belt. She'd have to find other ways of settling in and making the place hers. Likely, she'd find other treasures, which would mean something to her. Just as she had when she'd gone to live with her aunt in the big farmhouse.

She sat on her cot and heard paper crumple under her butt. Reaching beneath the blanket she pulled out a folded piece of paper. She opened it and read.

Stay safe and have fun planting seeds, sweetheart.

I know you have planted one in my heart.

Warren

Folding the paper up again and holding it to her heart, she thought Warren's favorite word. *Good.* It felt good to know she had a place in his heart. He would return. She began to grin.

A knock came on the door and Brandon said, "I thought you might be lonely now that Warren is gone. Want to come over and play checkers or backgammon? We're gathering at my place."

"Isn't your place kind of small?"

"Big enough for four men or women to sit and play. It's warm and cozy. You'll see. I'll bring out the candy I've been saving, if you're in. I have chocolate." He smiled with that last word, as if knowing the word chocolate would entice her.

"Okay, I'm in."

He glanced at the wall where the hip scarf hung. "Oh, hey that's cool. You dance?"

"I did."

"Nice. We'll have to play some music at our next barbeque. Sometimes the guys drum, and Hachi does the native American drum circle stuff. Vivaan plays more like a rhythm from a Bollywood movie and Suwanne has a native American flute. So, we have a mix of music here and much of it you could dance to if you like to dance."

"Oh, I would love that." Clarissa laughed. "I love to dance."

"See, it's not so bad living here." He handed her a poncho he'd kept folded up under his arm. "I even have rain gear for you."

"Oh, how nice." She took it from him. "Thank you."

"Well, put it on if you're ready."

"I'd like a moment first."

"Sure, take your time."

She reached for one of Warren's T-shirts he'd left for her and pulled it over her head. Then before she turned back to Brandon she tucked the folded note into the top of her sundress, to keep it close to her heart.

She pressed the note close to her breast and took a breath. She thought about the seed in Warren's heart, and how he'd also planted a seed in hers. She thought about how they would grow. She would treasure his note and one day he would return. Letting her hand drop down, she turned and moved toward Brandon ready for her next adventure to begin as she prepared to meet the others. "All right. I'm ready. Let's go."

THE END

NOTE FROM THE AUTHOR

Interesting facts I based this story on:

Since 2004, some hospitals have had the ability to implant humans to implant humans with chips the size of a grain of rice. The idea was to be able to monitor people with HIV and other diseases to prevent infecting others. RFID devices, or Radio Frequency Identification Devices, have also been implanted in animals and pets to allow the pin pointing of physical location by latitude, speed, and direction of movement. These chips have a sixteen-digit ID number for individual identification.

Could all humans in a country be chipped and tracked by their own government? Yes, of course. There would be no privacy, as your every move would be tracked, including your purchases, health history, and what drugs or chemicals are present in your body.

I hope that day never comes.

ALSO BY DEBRA PARMLEY

Hunger Roads Trilogy:
A Change of Scenery, book one
Down a Back Road, book two – 2018 release
Into the Convergence Zone, book three – 2018 release

Montana Marine: Brotherhood Protectors Kindle World series
To Catch an Elf: Pennsylvania Fighter Pilot - Nov. 2017 release

Isabella, Bride of Ohio, #17 in the American Mail Order Bride series

Butterflies Fly Free series:
Trapping the Butterfly, book one
Dancing Butterfly, book two – 2017 release

Check Out
Aboard the Wishing Star
Jenna's Christmas Wish
Dangerous Ties
A Desperate Journey
The Twelve Stitches of Christmas
Vague Directions

ABOUT THE AUTHOR

Debra Parmley spreads love, one story at a time. Fascinated by fairy tales and folktales ever since she was young, she has always ended her stories with a happy ever after. Damsel in distress stories are some of her favorites, and you will find this theme in many of her stories. Her westerns have been described as gritty.

Debra enjoys writing, reading, playing a medieval lady in the SCA (Society for Creative Anachronism) and world travel. Her work as a travel consultant gave her the opportunity to visit many countries and her luggage often carried home folk tales from the countries visited. Her three favorite things are dark chocolate, visiting the beach and ocean, and hearing from her readers. Each card, letter and email is a treasured gift, like finding a perfect shell upon the beach.

For more about Debra visit www.debraparmley.com

Made in the USA
Lexington, KY
24 November 2017